Puppet Master

Linda McNabb

Also by Linda McNabb

The Dragon's Apprentice
Shadow Hunters
Dragons' Bane

Circle of Dreams: Runeweaver
Circle of Dreams: Timeweaver
Circle of Dreams: Starweaver

Dragon Charmers: Mountains of Fire
Dragon Charmers: Valley of Silver
Dragon Charmers: Caverns of Gold
Dragon Charmers: Alyxa(Short Story)

Seventh Son

Stonekeeper's Daughter

Crystal Runners

Last Star

Maze Keepers

Realm of Shadows: The Guardian

Crown of Kings (with GJ Kelly)

Copyright Linda McNabb 2011

www.mcnabbnz.com

Linda McNabb asserts the moral right to be identified as the author of this work.

CHAPTER ONE
BABYSITTING A DRAGON

Jac threw the small armload of branches into the back of the wagon and climbed up onto the driving seat next to Danel. He flicked the reins and the sturdy old horse trotted obediently towards the line of wagons in the distance. The circus didn't travel slowly and they didn't wait for those on punishment duty as a day without a show meant a day without coin coming in.

'Not much there, Jac,' Danel commented as he slouched back against the low wooden board that separated them from the branches. 'Blyne'll be angry.'

'It's a bit hard to gather wood when there are hardly any trees or bushes,' Jac replied defensively as he looked around at the barren, windblown landscape. They were between towns and this was one of the largest stretches of plain in the lowlands. They hadn't even seen any animals for the last two days and Jac could understand why. It was only the beginning of winter and the ground was all but frozen. Not the sort of weather animals enjoyed and neither did Jac. In midwinter it was covered in drifts of snow so deep that horses would barely be able to walk.

'Hardly enough work for one, let alone two. I

think I'll have a snooze.' Danel grinned at Jac and then pulled his hat over his face to keep the wind off it.

'You've not done any yet,' Jac pointed out and poked his friend in the ribs.

'Ah, but you put the frogs in the girls' wagon.' Danel lifted his hat briefly. 'Becky sure can scream loud, Rosy too!'

'It was your idea, your sisters and your frogs,' Jac persisted and then gave up with a smile. 'Sure was funny to see them running through the camp screaming though.'

Jac turned the wagon towards another clump of small bushes and sat in silence as they bounced over the rocky plain. He stopped the horse when they reached the bushes and jumped down to gather wood. At least the effort of gathering wood was keeping him warm. Circus clothes definitely weren't designed for the cold weather. Muslin shirts and brightly coloured loose trousers were fine in the hot summers but the wind bit right through them out here in the plains.

They were back on the main south road, trying to catch up with the circus when the sound of hooves made him turn. It wasn't unheard of for bandits to attack out here.

Jac breathed a sigh of relief to see it definitely wasn't bandits. There was only one horse, riding at full trot, which didn't impress Jac at all. He knew the hard ground was bad for the horse's hooves and it might go lame if pushed too hard. The man who rode it didn't look as if he cared about horses though and his face was hard and angular.

'Danel!' Jac reached over and nudged his friend. 'Rider coming up fast.'

Danel sat up and pulled his hat off his face. Both boys reached into the back of the wagon and selected a stout branch, which they laid next to them as the rider pulled his mount up alongside.

'You there, boys.' The man's voice was like gravel rolling down a mountain.

'Yes?' Jac had to look up to see the man's face and it was clear that this man wasn't from around here. He was definitely too tall to be a dwarf and was dressed in black from head to foot, not a colour any local wore as they preferred bright colours.

'How far to the next town?' the man rasped, his black eyes boring into Jac and Danel as he brushed his windblown, mostly grey, hair from his face. It was a very unfriendly and sour stare that made Jac tighten his grip on the branch next to him.

'There's Drevon, a dwarf mining town, about a day's ride south. Then another day till you reach Sweetwater.' Jac was sure the man wasn't even listening as he stared at them while his horse kept pace noiselessly. Jac had a sudden feeling of danger that rippled through him.

The man broke eye contact with a brief nod of acknowledgement and slapped his horse cruelly with a leather whip.

'Weird eh?' Danel pushed his hat onto his head and stared after the rider.

'Just a traveller,' Jac said distantly. It was unlikely the man really wanted directions. If he wasn't from the lowlands then he must have come through the mountain pass to get here and that lay south of Sweetwater.

He looked like an elf, sort of, there were so many weird looking elves that it was sometimes hard to tell. There was a mix of elves and dwarves in Mr Blyne's circus, and of course Kimi, the dragon. Kimi was the only tame dragon that Jac knew of. Usually dragons were wild and lived far to the south in the huge desert beyond the highlands. They preferred to keep to themselves and were rarely seen.

Jac was the puppet master, which meant he made the puppets and ran the puppet shows for Mr Blyne's circus. He was considered a freak, here in the lowlands, since he was over five feet already at the age of twelve and he didn't look to have stopped growing yet. Danel was a good head shorter than Jac, which wasn't surprising since he was part dwarf but he was stoutly built and stronger than he appeared. He needed to be strong since he was in the trapeze act with his two sisters, Becky and Rosy.

The rider had already caught up with the circus wagons but rode past without pausing, kicking up great clouds of dust as he went. Jac knew they hadn't seen the last of him, he couldn't say how he knew, but he did.

The wagons rolled slowly to a complete stop just as the sun dipped near the mountains to the west. Jac gave the reins one last flick to bring the horse around next to the other wagons. With practised ease he jumped down from the high seat and unhitched the horse. One of the general hands came past and the horse trotted obediently after him, knowing that food and a rubdown was waiting.

Jac and Danel gathered up the wood they had collected and carried it over to the firepit that was being dug in the centre of the circle of wagons. Then they ran off around the back of the wagons before they could get roped into helping further.

'Jac.' His mother, Madame Zora, the fortune-teller, waved out to him as he passed a gap in the wagons. 'Gabbi wants to see you.'

'Okay,' Jac called back as he continued around the wagons. What could Gabbi want? She had avoided him ever since he and Danel had put fresh paint on the door handle of her wagon. That had been almost a year ago. She hadn't seen the funny side then and still didn't.

'I'll see you later,' Danel said as he saw his father waving at him across the camp. 'Keep out of trouble.'

Jac walked along the back of the wagons until he reached one that was slightly back from the others, not quite in the circle. It wasn't like any of the others as it had bars for sides and straw covering the floor. The bars had been raised at one end and the 'cage' was empty. To an untrained eye the roof of the wagon would look strangely misshapen but Jac knew differently. The 'roof' lifted a large scaly head and shiny golden eyes watched his progress towards the wagon.

'Hi Kimi, where's Gabbi?' Jac smiled up at the large golden dragon half-slumbering in the last rays of the sun.

Nearby, a voice in his head told him. Kimi sometimes spoke directly into his mind and he winked a thank you up to her.

'Over here,' Gabbi called as she emerged from behind the wagon. She was pulling her flame-red hair back into a ponytail, an act that made her look even less like a girl than usual. She was short, slim and she preferred to wear shirts and trousers rather than the soft, multicoloured muslin dresses that all the other circus women wore. It led most people to believe she was a young boy rather than a girl of almost thirteen. She had looked after Kimi alone since her mother passed away several years ago. Mr Blyne hadn't wanted such a young girl to be in charge of an important part of the circus but Kimi wouldn't allow anyone else to care for her.

'Kimi is looking good,' Jac commented, unsure how to ask what she wanted. He always felt tongue tied around Gabbi. Almost as if he was in awe of her even though she was less than a year older than him and half a handspan shorter. She was such a strong willed person and she always seemed to know exactly what she wanted out of life and how to get it.

'She always enjoys the sun,' Gabbi agreed with a smile for Kimi who rumbled and then tucked her head under her tail. Gabbi shuffled her feet in the dusty ground looking unsure of herself. Then she sighed, looking resigned to what she was about to do. 'I need you to watch Kimi for me tonight. I have to do something and I can't take her with me.'

'Me?' Jac couldn't help his surprise. Gabbi never let anyone else care for Kimi. What could be so important way out here in the barren wasteland?

'She won't let anyone else near her.' Gabbi

looked over at the quickly setting sun nervously. 'I promise I'll be back before dawn. She'll probably just sleep on the roof all night anyway.'

'Sure,' Jac agreed, not wanting to give her time to change her mind. 'Has she been fed?'

'Yesterday, so she won't bother the horses tonight.' Gabbi was edging backwards towards the back of the wagon as she spoke and seemed eager to leave. 'Just put her in the wagon if she's any bother.'

Jac just nodded as Gabbi disappeared out of sight. Kimi was never any bother; she just preferred to be alone.

Jac swung himself up onto the roof with ease. Filling in on the various acts, as he had to, had finely tuned his muscles. Kimi shifted one foreleg to make room for him and her long claws scraped on the wooden roof.

I'm not afraid of Ivan. Kimi spoke into his mind again. She sounded grumpy that she had been left behind. Jac was about to ask who Ivan was but her eyes were closed and her breathing slowed.

He lay down with his head resting on Kimi's scaly foreleg and looked up at the night sky. The first stars were just visible and he stared up at them, perfectly content to spend the night with Kimi up on the roof. It was cold but Kimi's warm body was enough to keep him comfortable. He could smell dinner cooking but he knew there would be plenty left over for breakfast so he'd eat then. He let his eyes slowly close and with Kimi snoring steadily next to him, he nodded off.

Jac stirred. Something on the edge of his mind invaded his sleep – and he fell. He'd had the sensation of falling just as he woke up many times before. Lately it had been almost every night but this time it hurt!

In his dream he was riding on Kimi, soaring through the clouds, dipping and diving on air currents with a flock of honking geese. Then one of the geese turned and hissed at him and he tumbled off Kimi and towards the ground.

Jac sat up, expecting to find that he had fallen off the roof of Kimi's wagon, but he hadn't. He rubbed his grazed elbow in confusion. Surely you couldn't be hurt in a dream, could you?

'Shhh!' a hissed command came from under the roof where he sat next to the lightly snoring dragon.

'What was that thump?' another voice whispered, sounding frightened.

'Who knows? Who cares? We've got other things to think about. We've gotta get my gem before that dragon gets back,' the first person hissed again.

Gems? That must mean that Kimi had been up to her old tricks again. She loved shiny stones and gems so much that she took any she could find and kept them. She guarded them fiercely and only a fool would try to steal them back. Usually the owner asked Gabbi to get them.

Obviously whoever it was in Kimi's wagon wasn't willing to wait until Gabbi returned. Jac tried to pick who it was by their voices but their whispering made them unrecognisable. Jac hoped Kimi didn't wake up while the men, for their voices were too low to be women, retrieved their precious stones. It didn't help that the main currency here in the lowlands was gems and precious stones as there were always lots of them about to tempt Kimi.

'Here they are. There are lots. Which one is it?' the second voice asked, a little too loudly, and Jac cast a nervous look at Kimi but she continued to snore peacefully.

'That one,' came the eager reply.

'Is it the Star Crystal?' the man's helper sounded excited yet nervous.

'Of course it's not you fool, crystals are clear. Besides, if I had the Star Crystal I wouldn't be hanging around this dump. I need the map before I can find it.' Scorn brought his voice just above a whisper and Jac strained to see if he could place the voice yet, but the drawl of the circus accent meant it could be almost anyone. Jac had never heard of a Star Crystal before and what was this map they were talking about?

'Why are you taking them all?' The helper's voice was moving away to the edge of the wagon and Jac heard several pairs of feet thud on the frozen ground.

'What does a dumb dragon need with gems?' The first one scoffed and their voices faded as they moved off.

Jac wriggled to the edge of the roof and caught a glimpse of the men's shadows as they disappeared around the side of the next wagon. One was taller than the other but that was all he could tell as their shadows were distorted by the flickering firelight coming from the centre of the circle of wagons.

Jac wondered if he should follow them to get Kimi's gems back. She had a few of her own that Gabbi had given her and she would be angry that they were gone. Jac didn't want to be around if Kimi got angry as she usually seared everything within a twenty-foot range with her fiery breath.

He hesitated, torn between following to retrieve her gems and the promise he'd made to Gabbi to stay with the dragon. He gently nudged Kimi but she didn't even falter in her steady rhythmic snoring and Jac made up his mind. He swung himself quietly down from the roof, wincing at the bruise he could feel forming on his right elbow. He'd have to figure that one out later!

Jac darted quickly between the wagons and went after the two men. All he had to do was see who it was and tell Gabbi. She'd sort them out.

He went around the wagon and skirted along the edge of the light from the dying fire, looking to see if he could spot two men walking together. It must be later than he thought as everyone appeared to have retired for the night.

Far across the circle he saw two people who fitted what he had seen and he hurried down the back of the wagons to cut them off. He could see them just up ahead and he slowed to a stalking pace as he worked his way towards them. They were leaning closely together, probably examining the gems, and in a few more steps Jac would be close enough to see who it was.

'That's one of them! Get him!'

Jac turned at the sudden, loud shout that came from behind him, out in the barren countryside. He couldn't make out any faces but he didn't need to. Trolls – and they were after him!

CHAPTER TWO
WATCH OUT FOR THE TROLLS

It took several seconds for Jac to realise that he hadn't moved. What were trolls doing out here? Bandits didn't usually attack a camp at night and the circus had little of value to take anyway. Maybe they weren't bandits? True, not all bandits were trolls and not all trolls were bandits but what did that leave? They were definitely attacking and they seemed to be after him.

'He fits the description. Tall, long dark hair and blue eyes. We'll get this one.' The troll who seemed to be in charge stopped a few steps in front of him. 'You three go get that other boy, brown spiky hair and a big nose.'

They had just described Danel! What could they want with him and Danel? Had they played a joke on some trolls back in the last town? He didn't remember having done so but they seemed to know what both of them looked like. The three trolls left their boss and two others in front of Jac who was trapped with his back to a wagon. He'd have to find out why they wanted him later but first he had to warn Danel and get some of the circus folk to help fight the trolls. He shot a look sideways but two men he had been following were gone.

Jac climbed nimbly up on top of the wagon then ran around the circle of roofs towards Danel's wagon. To his surprise he heard feet behind him on the wooden roofs. Trolls were not known for their agility or speed so the fact that they were only two steps behind him had Jac worried.

'Danel!' Jac yelled as he neared the blue and yellow wagon that was Danel's home. 'Danel! Get out of there.'

Jac was thumping the roofs as hard as he could with his feet as he leapt from one wagon to the next, hoping to wake the circus folk to come to his aid.

'What's going on up there?' a voice shouted, half-sleepy, half-angry at being woken up.

'Trolls!' Jac yelled without slowing his pace. He leapt to Danel's wagon but with the trolls so close behind him he didn't dare stop. He thumped the wagon with his feet and then leapt on to the next with the trolls now only one step behind.

People began to pour out of every wagon. Half were in their sleeping clothes but all were armed with a club or piece of iron. Jac ran out of wagons as he reached Kimi's wagon which wasn't quite in line with the others. He saw Kimi wasn't where he left her and he knew that meant he was in even more trouble. He couldn't stretch his stride far enough to reach the next wagon so he executed a graceful somersault and extended his arms to slow his descent as he fell from the sky for the second time that night.

Danel burst out of his wagon, rubbing his eyes, and looking surprised to see the campsite full of armed men and trolls. The trolls jumped down from the wagon, less gracefully, and dusted their clothes off as they joined the other three who had come out between the wagons.

'We must not leave without them,' the leader snarled as the other trolls gathered beside him.

Jac moved over to Danel and pulled him over to the armed circus folk who were advancing on the trolls. The troll leader's eyes followed them, as did all the other trolls, and the intensity of their gaze made Jac shiver.

'What do they want?' Danel muttered as they backed away. 'Why are they staring at us?'

'They want you and me,' Jac replied, not taking his eyes off the leader. 'Do you recognise any of them?'

'All trolls look the same to me,' Danel replied with a shrug. It was a typical dwarf remark since trolls were second class citizens and dwarves were brought up to consider themselves superior.

The trolls saw the gathered forces of the camp advancing on them but instead of backing away they pulled short clubs from their belts and moved steadily towards Jac and Danel. Just when it seemed there would be no choice but to fight there was a shriek from the sky. Everyone, including the trolls, looked up to see what had made such a horrible noise. Kimi, with Gabbi on her back, swooped down and with a hissing flame she charred the ground just in front of the trolls.

That was obviously a little more than the trolls had been willing to deal with for they turned, as one, and fled between the wagons. Nobody followed them for the circus folk were against violence and would only fight in defence. Now that the threat was leaving they all lowered their weapons.

'But what if they come back?' Danel asked with a quiver in his voice that Jac knew would be in his too if he spoke.

'I'll have Kimi watch for them,' Gabbi said as Kimi landed silently behind them. 'She'll let us know if there's any more trouble.'

'All right. Everyone back to bed. We've got an early start,' Mr Blyne, the ringmaster and owner of the circus, bellowed as he tucked his wooden club under his armpit. He looked more like a clown, dressed in his red-stripped pyjamas and wearing the black tophat that he was never without. Even with the hat on he was still under four feet tall and he stamped his foot when nobody moved. 'NOW!'

Everyone started to move off, muttering quietly amongst themselves as one of the general hands ran up to Mr Blyne.

'The horses are gone. Somebody cut the ropes.' He puffed as he spoke and pointed towards the far side of camp. 'I tried to catch them but they ran off when Kimi made that noise.'

'Trolls!' Mr Blyne made it sound like a swear word and then he whirled to look directly at Jac and Danel. 'They seemed very interested in you two. What did you do to them?'

'Nothing,' Jac squeaked in their defence although he wasn't totally sure about it. They had upset a few a last summer when they had greased the trolls' saddles, but that hardly seemed to warrant this sort of attack.

'You two can round up the horses. On your own.' Mr Blyne had turned red and his hands were clenching into fists. 'And I want them all back by morning!'

Mr Blyne turned on his heels, stalked off towards his wagon and slammed his door shut. Within a minute only Jac, Danel, Gabbi and Kimi were left and it didn't look as if trouble had finished with Jac yet.

'You were supposed to be watching Kimi!' Gabbi exploded at Jac, her arm resting protectively on the great beast's back.

'I was…' Jac started, meaning to explain about the gems but she didn't give him a chance.

'I came back and you were nowhere in sight,' Gabbi accused him with her free hand on her hip. 'I knew I couldn't trust you!'

'But…' Jac let his defence die before it left his lips. Gabbi had turned and was leading Kimi back to her wagon, her back stiff with anger.

'Looks like we're not going to get any more sleep tonight,' Danel commented as Jac watched Kimi lift elegantly and effortlessly onto the roof of her wagon.

'We might as well get started,' Jac said with a sigh as he headed across the camp towards where the horses had gone.

'But the trolls are out there,' Danel pointed out, following a step behind.

'And Mr Blyne is in here, and if we don't come back with the horses we'll be in even more trouble,' Jac assured him. He saw the door to his own wagon open and the tall, thin figure of his mother stood on the top step, watching but not speaking or coming down the steps. 'Zora probably won't let me back in until we've got them either.'

They reached the makeshift pen the horses had been in and found the general hand mending the rope fences.

'I'd like to help you round them up but it'll take

me ages to fix this,' he told them. 'They went that way. Here, you'll need this rope to bring them in.'

Jac and Danel nodded their thanks, took the offered rope, and walked quietly out into the dark night. The moon wasn't quite full but it gave off just enough light for them to see the ground ahead of them. Jac didn't really want to take a lantern in case the trolls were still hanging around nearby. He was still worried about why they had wanted them badly enough to be willing to fight a whole circus troupe. The two of them on their own out here would have no chance against six trolls.

They came across the first two horses quickly, as Jac expected, for they were tame animals, born and bred into the circus and they hadn't wandered far. The horses were chewing a clump of the sparse wild grasses five minutes out from camp.

'That's two, only ten more to go,' Danel remarked dryly as they mounted. 'At least if those trolls come back we can ride back to camp now.'

Jac grunted his agreement for he too had been watching shadows near every bush they passed. The moon was about to set when they still had two horses to find and they circled to the other side of the camp to search there. It brought them closer to the direction the trolls had gone but they had no choice. Each leading four of the horses they slowly moved out in an increasing circle knowing that there were only a few hours before dawn.

A small camp fire up ahead in the distance made them both stop and they drew up next to each other to look at the small yellow light it gave off.

'What do you think?' Danel asked, keeping a firm hold on the horses.

'Might be the trolls, might not,' Jac replied and Danel scowled at him.

'That's a big help. Do we go near it or miss out that area?' he queried but then the sound of whinnying horses up ahead answered for Jac.

'I guess we have to go and take a look,' Jac said with a gulp. If they went back with two less horses Mr Blyne would dock their cut of the takings for months, maybe years. 'But keep downwind.'

There really wasn't any wind to keep downwind of but they dismounted, tied the horses to a large bush and crept forward, keeping low in the wild grass. They crawled as close as they dared, ready to jump up and run at the first sight or sound of trolls, and stopped at a small bush a few feet from the camp. They could hear nothing but the occasional snort from a horse and they peered through the branches of the bush.

'No trolls,' Danel whispered.

'Look it's the old mime guy,' Jac said softly as he pointed to the old man who sat on a rock next to the fire. The mime was a traveller, like the circus, and nobody knew what his real name was as he never spoke and he entertained crowds with his mimes. Jac often saw him in the same towns as the circus and in the highlands too. He certainly wasn't a threat to them.

'And he's got the last two horses,' Danel said a little louder now that they knew they weren't in danger. Jac looked where Danel was pointing and sure enough the two horses were tethered to a bush a few feet past the fire. 'Let's go get them.'

Both boys stood up and walked towards the fire, making sure the old man saw them before they got too close. There was no need to frighten him.

'Excuse me, Sir,' Jac said quietly as they approached and the old man looked up with startling blue eyes, made more intense by the reflection of the small fire. His face was heavily lined and what hair he had left was snow-white and unkempt. An untidy beard completed the image of a wandering beggar but his eyes showed an intelligence that did not seem to fit. He had a threadbare blanket drawn around his shoulders, covering most of his dirty and patched clothes but leaving his bare feet exposed. There were two tin cups sitting on the rock next to him and Jac looked around in the firelight to see who else was with him, but saw nobody.

'You have our horses, Sir,' Danel pointed at the two mares and the old man just nodded.

'May we take them back?' Jac wasn't used to a one-sided conversation but the old man swept his arm in a motion that Jac took to mean he should take them away.

Danel moved forward to take the horses and he was leading them away when Jac noticed that one of the tin cups had gone. He hadn't seen the old man move it, perhaps he had been mistaken and there had only been one all along.

'Thank you for holding them for us.' Jac nodded in a short bow and as he did he heard a voice.

Watch out for the trolls, the archmage sent them.

He snapped his head back up and stared at the old man, but he still had the serene smile that told Jac the voice had not come from his lips. So who had said it? Jac looked nervously around the edges of darkness that were creeping closer to the fire as the moon sank below the horizon. He looked back at the old man and his eyes seemed different now, more serious and a little annoyed.

'Come on Jac, it'll be light in an hour,' Danel called to him in a voice loud enough that showed he didn't consider them to be in danger any more. Jac wasn't so sure as he backed away from the old man, keeping eye contact as he did. He didn't seem as harmless as he had a few seconds ago.

Jac mounted one of the horses and rode off without looking back. His heart was beating loud enough to block out the horse's hooves as he led them back towards camp and the safety it promised.

They penned the horses and were about to collapse with exhaustion when the first of the wagon doors opened and the campfire was stoked up. A new day in the circus had begun and there would be no time for sleep now. Jac sank down next to the fire, hoping that a bowl of leftovers from last night would give him the energy to get through the day. Danel collapsed on the other side and his eyes shut as he hit the ground.

'You found all the horses?' Madame Zora sat down next to Jac, tucking her long muslin dress around her legs and rubbing them for warmth. She had a colourful scarf covering most of her curly black hair and her face looked pale and drawn. She regarded him with a stern look for a second and then pulled his head over to lean on her shoulder. 'Jac, you know someday your pranks are going to cause you trouble you'll not be able to get out of.'

'Yes, Zora,' Jac muttered, knowing better than to argue with her. He wasn't worried that she was predicting his future either as he knew it wasn't possible. His mother didn't have any real magical talents, nobody, not even the magician of the troupe did. Jac had seen how all the tricks were done and they held no mystery for him.

'You two boys are in the wood wagon again.' Albot, Mr Blyne's son, came over to the fire and spoke with a taunting voice. Albot was almost the same height as the ringmaster but even when Jac was sitting down he was nearly as tall as Albot. He wore a top hat like his father's but it wasn't as tall. Albot knew the circus would one day be his but he acted as if it were already. 'You'd better get more than you did yesterday.'

Madame Zora put a warning hand on Jac's shoulder as he felt his anger rise. Albot walked off, ordering people around as he went and Jac glared after him.

'Jumped up little…' Jac muttered and Madame Zora shook her head in dismay as she got up and went to hitch a horse to her wagon.

The food didn't do much to wake him up and an hour later when the circus broke camp he was finding it hard to stay awake. The wood wagon rumbled out last with Jac at the reins and Danel sitting next to him.

'How about we take turns sleeping in the back,'

Danel suggested and at Jac's brief nod he jumped over the seat and lay down before Jac could ask to go first.

Jac steered the horse onto the main north road and let the reins go slack. He knew the horse would follow the other wagons and his chin dropped to his chest as his eyes blinked shut.

'Jac!'

His eyes flew open as he felt someone grab his shirt and tug him from behind. He twisted around; ready to hit out if it was a troll.

'Jac, another wagon train is coming up behind us.' Danel was sitting in the back of the open wagon, still bare of wood, staring at the fast approaching wagons.

Was it the trolls again? Or this archmage he had been warned about last night? He didn't even know what one was. Jac looked up ahead and saw they were not far from the rest of the circus. He slapped the reins against the horse and it stepped up the pace. If they were lucky they would catch up to the circus wagons before the others reached them.

Jac flicked the reins again, his heart racing. He kept glancing back from the safety that lay ahead as he tried to see who drove the wagons behind him.

CHAPTER THREE
TWO FRIENDS LIKE DANEL

They caught up to the rest of the circus just as the first of the approaching wagons came close enough for Jac to see the driver. He felt the tension drain away instantly when he saw a dwarf at the reins. If there was a dwarf on the lead wagon then there wouldn't be any trolls with them at all.

Dwarves didn't tolerate trolls. Mr Blyne made exceptions in the mining camps and some small towns because there was nobody else to come to his show but usually the two races kept their distance.

Jac recognised the dwarf as the leader of a local troupe of entertainers. As locals they didn't go through the mountain pass and stayed in the lowlands all year round. Not many people knew about the mountain pass and Mr Blyne wanted it kept that way. The penalty for telling anyone was to be cast out of the circus. They were the only troupe to travel to both the highlands and the lowlands and the ringmaster wanted it to stay that way. The dwarf troupe usually worked different towns to the circus in the lowlands but every now and then they met up. Mr Blyne didn't like them at all because it halved his takings when they were in town.

'I wonder where they're going in such a hurry,' Danel mused as he climbed up front and sat next to Jac.

'I doubt whether they'd want to stop the night at Drevon, since it's populated mostly by trolls, so they must be trying to make it to Sweetwater by nightfall,' Jac guessed and Danel nodded in agreement.

'Either that or they've heard about the royal wedding too,' Danel commented with a yawn.

'Blyne won't be pleased to have competition. He wanted to be the entertainment at the wedding,' Jac laughed.

The king of the lowlands was marrying off his youngest daughter and the wedding was in a few weeks. A huge crowd would be in Sweetwater for the wedding and Mr Blyne was not one to miss a chance to make an easy pile of gems. Then, hopefully, they would go north again to the warm weather. They normally didn't come this far south until the winter was well and truly over. The cold was strength sapping at the best of times. Jac preferred the warmth but where the circus went so did he and his mother.

'Your turn for a sleep,' Danel said as he took the reins and pulled the wagon off the road again, heading for a small clump of trees. 'I'll get the wood today.'

Jac didn't argue and he climbed onto the back tray of the wagon and curled up in a corner, knocking his sore elbow as he did so. He still hadn't worked that out but he was too tired now. He nodded off easily to the gentle swaying of the wagon, not noticing when it stopped for Danel to collect wood, and he didn't wake up until the wagon rolled into Drevon.

'We're here already?' Jac sat up and rubbed his eyes, being careful not to scratch himself on the wood piled all around him. Danel had certainly been busy as there was twice the amount they gathered yesterday. He looked at the sun, deciding it was about three or four hours till sunset.

'Yep,' Danel replied, concentrating on keeping the horse steady as they followed a deep-rutted track that led into the mining town.

Jac extracted himself from the firewood and joined Danel up front. The only industry in Drevon was mining, in mines owned by the dwarves. They reached the centre of town, a barren, rocky field with a wooden shack at one side. It was the general store for the town and sold anything that the trolls needed, if they could pay for it. It was, of course, run by a dwarf.

Danel had to stop the wagon to let a group of trolls cross on their way back from the mines. Their clothes might well have been brightly coloured before going into the mines but the heavy woollen garments were dusty and streaked with mud now. For a brief second Jac felt a wave of fear at the sight of the trolls. Were the trolls who had attacked them in town? And what did an archmage look like? Was it some sort of leader of the trolls? But the group passed by without any of them even looking up and Jac relaxed again, feeling a little foolish for suspecting the miners.

They lined the wagons up along the back of the rocky field, not in a circle as they had in the barren lands. Then everyone fell to the task of erecting the bigtop. It was exhausting work and if it wasn't for Kimi's help in raising the roof it would be almost impossible.

Jac had just finished putting his puppet theatre together and there was an hour before the show. He went in search of his mother and found her setting up her fortune telling stall.

'What's an archmage?' Jac asked casually as he helped drape the purple material over the frame of her stall. She had a shawl draped over her shoulders as it was even colder up here in the mountains.

'Where did you hear that word?' Mme Zora asked, throwing him a yellow star to pin above the door.

'I... I'm not sure,' Jac replied. It wasn't a lie

because he didn't know if it was the old man or just his own mind playing tricks on him.

'There's no such thing. It was the name given to wizards of extraordinary powers in the years long ago. But that's all just stories. I've told you before there's no such thing as magic.' His mother continued decorating her stall without even looking at him and Jac wandered off.

He went back to his puppet theatre and put up a sign which showed the sun setting over a mountain. There was no point in putting a time on the sign as nobody in Drevon could read. Then he walked around the back of the wagons, found a quiet spot, and sat down to rest for a few minutes.

It was fully dark by the time Jac stirred and felt the usual thump as fell from his dream. He knew instantly that he had missed doing his puppet show. He got up and shivered. He walked out to the front of the wagons and saw that the whole field was lit with lanterns on top of poles. One thing a mining town was never short of was lanterns.

Jac faintly heard the music strike up over in the red and white stripped bigtop and knew that the performance had started. He decided it was probably best to keep out of the way until afterwards and then find a way to explain about the missed puppet show. Just as he reached his red and green wagon he saw Danel running across the well-lit field towards him.

'Here,' Danel said and thrust a tangled mess of wooden puppets into his arms. 'I filled in for you so Blyne'll never know you weren't there. Gotta go, I'm on next.'

'Thanks Danel,' Jac called out to him as he ran back towards the bigtop. Danel might be full of mischief but he was a good friend. He opened the door and went inside then lit a lamp and put the puppets back in their box. There was nothing for him to do until the end of the show today, when he had to go and start collapsing the tent ready for their departure in the morning. Sometimes he had to fill in on one of the acts but nobody was sick or injured right now.

He picked up a chunk of wood that he had found several weeks ago. He'd been saving it to make his next puppet but hadn't found the time. Now was as good as any, he guessed, and hunted through his box of puppet parts. Before long he had the body completed, dressed in a pair of loose red leggings and soft muslin shirt, held across the hips with a leather strip. He just had to carve a head from the chunk of wood. He sat and stared at it, wondering what face he should carve it into. Lately he'd been making them to look like the mayor in each town and it had raised a laugh among the townspeople. He seemed to have a natural skill in carving and the faces were easy for him to do.

The bump in the middle of it reminded him of a large nose and he smiled, Danel. He took out his carving tools and bent to his task. It was some hours later that the noise outside intruded on his work. He looked out the window and saw the tent was being packed away. He knew he had to get out there and help for he would surely be missed this time. The head was almost finished, all he had to do was chisel in the dimple on the left cheek and it would be a perfect image of Danel. Danel would be surprised when he showed him. He carefully chiselled out the dimple then put the head onto the body.

'Shame you're not real as I could do with two friends like Danel,' Jac mused as he opened the door.

Jac chuckled to himself as he shut the door behind him. Anyone listening would think he was crazy, talking to a puppet!

It was well after moonrise when the tent was finally packed away and the site cleared up.

'Hey Danel, I've got something to show you,' he said to Danel as they parted company at Danel's wagon.

'I'm stuffed. I'll catch up with you tomorrow,' Danel replied, rubbing his arms to warm himself up as he hurried off.

'Sure,' Jac agreed and carried on walking.

He saw his mother heading over towards Mr Blyne's wagon. Jac knew she didn't really like the little dwarf so it wouldn't be a social call. He wondered what it could be about since it was so late but he figured he'd find out if his mother wanted him to know. Gabbi had been prowling around the whole time they were packing the tent, as if she were looking for something. Jac had made sure he kept well out of her way because she didn't look as if she was having any luck finding whatever it was and she wasn't looking at all happy.

His step faltered as he approached his wagon when he saw Danel staring out the side window. Jac frowned and then laughed as he realised it was just the puppet. He must have left it propped up against the window when he left in such a hurry earlier. He opened the door and saw that he had left the lamp lit. It was just as well his mother wasn't first back or he'd be in big trouble, again.

'Jac gone long time. Dan worried!' Danel's voice came from just behind him and almost made him knock the lamp over as he turned down the flame.

'Danel?' Jac turned, expecting to find that Danel had followed him in but there was nobody there. Great, more voices in his head to drive him crazy!

'Dan, not Danel,' the voice chirped up. It was definitely Danel's voice and Jac's eyes darted all around the room looking for him. There weren't many places to hide in the small wagon as it was one room with curtains for dividing it at night.

'Where are you? I give up.' Jac said with a chuckle. This sure was the best trick he'd played for a while.

'Here,' Danel's voice was right behind him and Jac turned but still did not see him. The only thing there was the puppet he had made earlier. Jac leaned down to look at the puppet. He was sure it had been facing the window when he came in but now it was looking right at him.

'Jac looks tired.'

Jac stared at the puppet for several seconds and then his face drained of all colour and he stepped back in horror as he realised it had spoken.

'Who are you?' Jac demanded, feeling ill.

'Dan. Told you that before,' he replied with a cheeky grin. 'Now you have two friends like Danel.'

'Two friends like Danel...' he muttered to himself as he ran over what he had said, and done, earlier. He remembered saying that as he left the wagon but that was all he remembered. 'But you're a puppet!'

Jac shook his head, screwed up his eyes and then opened them again but the puppet was still there and it waved a short, wooden arm at him.

'Not any more. Jac make me real.' The puppet pointed one skinny finger at him, and Jac sank into a chair, speechless.

'How?' Jac asked Dan, not really believing that he was talking to a puppet.

Dan just shrugged and raised one eyebrow at Jac. Jac shook his head in disbelief and rubbed his temples, he was getting a headache.

'But magic isn't real,' Jac persisted, refusing to believe what his eyes were seeing.

'Isn't it?' Dan sounded surprised. 'Then how did I get here?'

'I...' Jac frowned as the puppet looked at him with trusting, 'real' eyes. Dan looked like a puppet but he was moving and talking and obviously capable of thinking for himself. In short, he was alive. 'I have no idea.'

'I think I will like it here.' The puppet turned and moved jerkily to look out the window where Jac had seen him a few minutes ago. 'Circus looks like fun. Can I ride the dragon?'

Jac stood behind Dan and looked out at Gabbi leading Kimi over to her wagon for the night. Normally Kimi was 'locked up' well before this time of night. Trolls were uneasy about having a dragon roaming free in their town. Where had she been?

'Lady coming!' Dan cried, jumping up and

down on the seat of the chair he was standing on. He was far too short to see out the window without it.

Jac looked, realising it was his mother and felt a wave of panic. What was he going to do with Dan? She told him there was no magic only a few hours ago so this would come as a shock to her. As she got closer he could see she was looking tired and he decided that tonight wasn't the best time to spring this sort of thing on her.

'You've got to hide,' Jac ordered, grabbing Dan by the hand and was more than a little surprised to find that it was warm.

'Why?' Dan asked obstinately and pouted like a small child.

'That's my mother, Madame Zora, and she lives here too…' Jac began but Dan interrupted him.

'With us?' Dan looked delighted.

'With… us, I suppose. Anyway, my point is that she doesn't like surprises and I need to find a way to tell her about you.' Jac dragged Dan to where his bed was in the far corner of the wagon and pushed him under it.

'But I want to meet mother!' Dan crawled out and stood with his hands on his hips, pouting angrily.

'Hurry up and get under there or I'll… take you apart again,' he threatened but when Dan's face dissolved into a look of shock and fear he backed off a bit. 'Just get under there.'

Dan crept under, sobbing quietly, but it was still loud enough that Mme Zora would hear.

'Shhh...' Jac hissed but Dan kept sobbing. Jac frantically tried to think of something that would cheer the puppet up. 'If you keep quiet I'll take you to see the dragon tomorrow.'

Dan fell silent instantly, only a split second before Madame Zora opened the wagon door and came in.

'You still up, Jac?' she asked, a little surprised. 'What've you been doing?'

'Umm... this and that,' Jac replied evasively. 'I think I'll turn in now.'

'Night then, see you in the morning.' His mother smiled at him but Jac could see something was bothering her.

Jac shut the curtain and lay on his bed, feeling more exhausted than he had after rounding up the horses. Dan crawled out from under the bed and climbed onto it, resting his head on the pillow with a sigh, before a gentle snore said he was asleep. Jac lay staring at the ceiling, wondering how all of this would change his life.

CHAPTER FOUR
DO YOU BELIEVE IN MAGIC?

Jac woke with the strangest feeling, just as the sun coloured the sky with a tinge of pink. Something was pushing down on his stomach and he cautiously opened one eye to see what it was.

'Jac awake. Morning now. Why Jac float in his sleep?' Dan crawled up Jac's chest and peered into his open eye with a keen interest.

The events of the previous evening came flooding back and he opened his other eye to return Dan's inquisitive stare. It hadn't been a dream after all! The little puppet grinned at him and jumped up to stand on his chest.

'See dragon now?' he asked excitedly as he peered out the window.

Jac knew something wasn't quite right, apart from the fact a puppet was jumping on his chest. The window by his bed was near the roof of the wagon and Jac could only just see out of it when he was standing on his bed, so how could the puppet see out it? Something Dan had said a minute ago finally sank in and Jac sat up and hit his head of the roof, nearly sending the puppet flying. He was floating up near the roof of the wagon and he stared at the huge gap between him and the bed.

'What?' Jac exclaimed as he rubbed his head and felt himself slowly sinking down to the bed.

There was no comment from out beyond the curtain at his sudden shout so Jac assumed that his mother must have already left the wagon.

'Fun!' Dan cried in delight as he clung to Jac's shirt with one wooden hand, swinging gently from side to side. 'Again?'

'Not if I can help it,' Jac muttered as his feet finally touched the floor.

He grabbed hold of Dan and put him firmly on the bed and then pulled the curtain aside. He had to go and help his mother get ready to leave, but what could he do with Dan?

'Stay here, I'll be back in a while,' Jac ordered, firmly but gently. 'You can watch out the window but stay out of sight.'

'Why?' Dan asked, looking up with wide trusting eyes, not at all like Danel's. The puppet might look like him, but it had the mind of a small child.

'Just because...' Jac muttered, wondering why he was suddenly reminded of his own childhood.

'Okay,' Dan said agreeably and jumped off the bed with his wooden limbs clicking and clacking in a very disturbing way. He ran over to a chair, climbed up and pressed his hard wooden nose against the glass. 'See the dragon soon?'

'Soon,' Jac promised and he slipped quickly out of the door before Dan decided he wanted to come as well. He breathed a sigh of relief when there was no wooden clicking to indicate that Dan was running for the door and he jumped down the steps in one leap.

His mother had collected their horse from the groomer and was heading back across the rocky field as he came around the front of the wagon. She looked just as grim and tired as last night and Jac immediately ran over and took the horse from her.

'I'll hitch up,' he offered and she didn't resist but followed him over and watched while he quickly attached the reins.

'We need to talk,' she said bluntly as if she had wanted to say it for some time.

'Now?' Jac looked at the wagons beginning to pull out of the field.

'It's important,' Madame Zora said, her face totally expressionless. She appeared to be looking at something far distant beyond Jac and he turned, hoping it wasn't Dan. He couldn't see him from here and he turned back as she continued. 'We're leaving the circus.'

'Leaving the circus!' Jac repeated, totally shocked. He had never expected they would leave, ever. They had been part of Blyne's Travelling Circus since he was only just able to walk. 'And go where?'

'I'm not sure yet.' A frown crossed her face and her eyes came back into focus as she stared hard at Jac. 'But we have to go. You're not safe here.'

'Not safe?' Jac felt like a parrot, repeating everything, but he couldn't help it.

'The less you know the better,' his mother said with an expression that told Jac she thought she had said too much already.

'Zora.' Jac knew this wasn't really the time to tell her about Dan but it would probably never be the right time. 'What if magic was real?'

'I've told you it's not!' she snapped, her green eyes flaring with anger so suddenly that Jac almost took a step back.

He hadn't expected such a dramatic response but he gulped, gathered his courage, and continued.

'Would it be so bad if it was?' he asked with as innocent a look as he could force.

'It would be a disaster. Don't even think about magic. Ever!' Madame Zora climbed onto the wagon seat and took the reins. 'We leave the circus after the wedding in Sweetwater.'

She flicked the reins and the horse trotted off, leaving Jac standing staring after the wagon. Why had she acted like that? Surely magic wasn't that bad? He saw Dan staring out the window as it clattered over the rocks, he didn't seem like a disaster. Dan's face disappeared and the back door opened. Jac broke into a run and caught up with the wagon just as Dan was about to leap off it.

'I told you to stay in the wagon,' Jac admonished him gently as he only just caught the puppet before he hit the ground. He didn't know if Dan would have been hurt but he didn't really want to find out.

'Dan stay with Jac,' he stated simply as he clung to Jac's shirt and smiled happily.

Jac didn't have the heart to be angry with the little puppet, besides with the mood his mother was in it was probably better if they both stayed away.

Albot came striding across the field with his chest puffed out like a mating seabird and waved at Jac to get his attention.

'Let's play a game,' Jac suggested to Dan, deciding that treating him like a child might just work.

'I like games,' he replied looking excited.

'Let's see if we can get this little man to think you're just a wooden puppet. Stay really still, okay?' Jac explained quickly, talking out the side of his mouth so that Albot wouldn't see his mouth moving as he got closer.

Dan nodded once, mischief in his eyes as his features relaxed into a blank expression.

'Jac, you're on the wood wagon again. It'll keep you out of trouble.' It was said in a bossy manner that was intended to raise Jac's anger but Jac just nodded.

'Fine,' he said without taking any offence.

In fact it suited him perfectly. He could keep Dan well out of sight all day while he taught him how to act around people. Dan was staying perfectly still and Jac wondered if the puppet needed to blink. Albot looked briefly at Dan and then back at Jac without a change in expression.

'Make sure you get a full wagon,' he ordered, not looking happy that he hadn't made Jac angry.

Jac simply nodded and wandered off towards the wood wagon, holding a limp Dan as he would any of his other puppets, swinging loosely in one hand. He reached the open wagon and jumped up to the seat, carefully placing Dan next to him.

'Fun!' Dan exclaimed, turning his face up to look at Jac.

'Shh! Here comes someone else. We'll play again okay?' Jac held one finger to his mouth as Danel came sauntering up to him.

'Albot really doesn't like you,' Danel said with a laugh. 'What did you ever do to him?'

'I don't mind. I think I'd be better off out of Zora's way today,' Jac replied, trying not to glance at Dan to see if he was staying still. As soon as Danel wasn't looking his way he would hide him in the back.

'I'll keep you company,' Danel offered. 'I'll only get to look after Rosy if I stay with our wagon.'

'But you did it all yesterday,' Jac said, a little too quickly. If Danel came with him he'd have trouble keeping him from seeing Dan.

'We'll take turns.' Danel jumped up, grabbed the reins and flicked them to start the horse across the field. 'You said you had something to show me.'

He looked down and immediately saw the puppet and grabbed it in one hand, pulling it up to take a closer look. To Jac's relief Dan stayed limp and lifeless. He was so convincing that Jac actually wondered if he had gone back to being just a puppet.

'Wow!' Danel grinned as he poked and prodded the puppet and then held it next to his own face. 'It looks just like me. This is neat Jac.'

Jac didn't comment. He was trying to work out how to get Dan off him and put him out of sight. He didn't know why he didn't want Danel to know that Dan was alive but he guessed that he would probably react like his mother.

'How'd you get the eyes to follow you?' Danel asked as he drove the wagon with one hand and the other was moving Dan side to side in front of him.

'Umm… It's a trade secret,' Jac replied and then cringed as he saw Dan blink twice. Jac remained calm as he waited to see if Danel had noticed, maybe he hadn't?

'Jac?' Danel held the puppet as far away from him as he could. 'It blinked!'

Dan's bland expression dissolved into a cheeky giggle and his hands came up to cover his mouth. Danel almost dropped the puppet and Jac grabbed Dan and then took the reins as well. Danel wasn't looking very well.

'Good game,' Dan said as he settled himself comfortably on Jac's knee. He pointed one long wooden finger at Danel and smiled. 'He looks like Dan.'

'Jac?' Danel repeated, looking nervously from the puppet to his friend and then back again. He had edged away as far as he could without falling off the seat. 'What is it?'

'A puppet,' Jac replied with a sigh. 'Do you believe in magic?'

'No!' Danel said with a very surprised look.

'Jac made me real,' Dan replied for him. 'He floats too.'

'Floats?' Danel parroted.

'In my sleep,' Jac replied. He hadn't wanted to tell anyone that just yet but Dan didn't seem to have any sense of what he should and should not say. 'It's only been the last few weeks.'

'Who else knows about... Dan?' Danel asked, still keeping his distance and watching Dan's every move suspiciously.

'Nobody, I tried to tell Zora but she went crazy when I suggested magic might be real. I decided it might be better if I didn't tell her just yet.'

'Parents. Who can figure them out,' Danel said as he slid a little closer on the seat. 'He won't bite will he?'

'Of course not,' Jac snorted as the wagon rumbled onto the main south road at the rear of the wagon train again. He was glad they had left at first light so there was nobody to watch them leave. He didn't want anyone else seeing Dan just yet, if ever.

They fell silent as they travelled along the dusty road, Dan sat happily in Jac's lap and Danel looked over every now and then to stare at him. Jac didn't bring up the fact that he was going to be leaving the circus soon. He hoped his mother would change her mind before the wedding and they would be able to stay. He wondered why she had said he wasn't safe, if he could do magic he would be able to keep himself safe from most things. That is, if he had someone to teach him how to use it.

They stayed well behind the rest of the circus, collecting wood, and when they rolled into Sweetwater late that afternoon Dan had been asleep in the back of the wagon for several hours. Danel was now used to seeing Dan move without wanting to leap off the wagon and his attention had turned to Jac's new talent.

'Are you going to make the rest of the puppets come alive?' Danel asked as they manoeuvred the wagon down the narrow cobbled street. Sweetwater was by far the largest town in the lowlands and dwarf children were running alongside the circus wagons, crying with delight at the unexpected visit from the circus.

'The rest?' Jac hadn't even considered the idea. 'I don't think so.'

'Then you could just sit back and they would do the puppet show all by themselves,' Danel explained, ever the lazy person, looking for the quickest way to do anything.

'And how would I keep a dozen of them...' he pointed towards the snoring Dan, 'out of Zora's sight.'

'Point taken,' Danel agreed and fell silent. Jac knew he was probably dreaming up some other scheme to use his magic for.

They rumbled noisily into the centre of town where a huge field lay not far from the castle. It was the best spot in town and since Mr Blyne was trying to catch the king's eye it was exactly the place to be. Just as the field came into view Jac could almost hear Mr Blyne yelling from the front of the wagon train. The troupe of dwarves who had passed them yesterday was set up right at the front of the field. They had spread out their tents and wagons so that they took up the whole road frontage of the field which was exactly what Mr Blyne usually did.

The only space left was at the back of the field, near the stream that flowed from the mountains up at Drevon and Jac knew it wasn't a good spot. The wagon train came to a halt as Mr Blyne had a loud, angry conversation with the leader of the dwarf troupe and then the circus rumbled on to the back of the field, completely hidden from view and near the pungent river.

Jac woke Dan up after he and Danel had unloaded the wagon and helped set up the bigtop. Danel had reluctantly gone to his own wagon after promising not to tell anyone about Dan. The little puppet yawned and stretched sleepily and then grinned at Jac. He hadn't asked for food at all so Jac had concluded that he didn't need to eat, which made things easier all round.

'See dragon now?' he asked eagerly.

'I guess so,' Jac replied, realising that he couldn't put it off forever. 'But if we see anyone you're to play that game again.'

Jac carried Dan over to where Kimi's wagon was, at the far end of the field, as far from the bigtop as possible. Jac was large compared to the dwarfs and Kimi was gigantic so she had to be kept well away so she didn't frighten them.

'Kimi, are you awake?' Jac called up to the shiny golden form on top of the roof.

'She's asleep.' A blunt, unfriendly voice informed him and he turned to see Gabbi standing by the corner of the wagon. Dan was playing his game well and Jac let him hang limply at his side.

'I'll come back later,' Jac offered, seeing that Gabbi didn't look at all happy to see him. She sure carried a grudge for a long time.

'We need to talk,' she said as she moved forward quickly and grabbed hold of his arm.

'Now?' Jac would rather put it off until he had put Dan away in the wagon and when Gabbi was in a better mood.

'It's important,' she assured him.

He seemed to remember hearing the same thing from his mother that morning and he hoped it was nothing as serious as her news had been.

'Come around the back where nobody can hear us,' she demanded and pulled him around the wagon without letting go of his arm. As soon as they were out of sight she turned to face him, angry and bitter. 'You can't hide it any longer!'

CHAPTER FIVE
THE PUPPET SHOW

'Hide what?' Jac asked, he wished people would stop talking in riddles today. Why couldn't they just say what they meant?

'I know what you are, grandfather told me,' Gabbi almost spat at him. 'He could feel it as soon as you were near him.'

'He could?' Jac didn't even know she had a grandfather, and he had certainly never met him, but now didn't seem the time to discuss relatives.

'It's been his life, watching out for people like you,' Gabbi said angrily. 'We can't have you just wandering around like you are. Goodness knows what trouble you'll get us all into!'

'What are you talking about?' Jac asked, confused and a little annoyed that she was yelling at him. 'I don't know who you think I am but I'm just Jac, the puppet master.'

'Just Jac?' Gabbi's voice had an undercurrent of hysterical laughter that made Jac shiver. 'If only.'

'What is it to you anyway?' Jac demanded.

'You know very well, you and your mother. Just like my grandfather, it's my job to look out for your sort and keep the world… and you, safe. A job that would have been far easier if you hadn't kept it hidden for so long.' Gabbi glared at him and Jac realised that she meant every word and that scared him.

'I can look after myself,' Jac said, thinking that he would learn to use his magic to protect himself, but protect himself from what?

'With magic?' Gabbi said sarcastically. 'You know that's not allowed. Surely your mother has told you what would happen if you did? It would be a disaster!'

Jac didn't know what to say in answer to that. It was clear that Gabbi knew about his magic, but how? And she seemed to think that his mother knew as well. Did she? And what awful thing was going to happen, for he'd already used his magic? She had used Zora's exact words to describe magic as well. It didn't sound as if anyone would think magic was a good thing.

'Just make sure you don't use it.' Gabbi obviously took his silence to mean she was right. 'Then we can all live a long and peaceful life. Anyway Grandfather will fix it as soon as he can.'

Gabbi strode off and left him standing behind the wagon on his own staring at the murky waters of the river. There were so many questions running around unanswered, not the least being Gabbi saying she had to look after 'his sort'. Were there more who could make puppets come alive? And just what was her grandfather going to fix?

'Angry lady,' Dan said softly, and Jac realised

the little puppet was shaking. 'Am I bad?'

'No, of course not,' Jac assured him, holding him closer for comfort. For whose comfort he wasn't sure but Dan seemed to like it and the shaking stopped.

'Jac bad for making me?' Dan kept pushing the subject, obviously having understood some of what Gabbi had said.

'Some people seem to think so, but I don't. What harm could you do? One small puppet surely isn't a threat to anyone.' Jac reassured him and Dan smiled a trusting and happy smile.

Jac kicked a stone into the river and it disappeared as soon as it plopped into the slow flowing, smelly water. Sweetwater. It wasn't a very well named town as the water was anything but sweet. Up in the mountains it ran clear and pure, but somewhere on the way down it was tainted, thickened and polluted. Jac had often wondered what it was that did it but short of following the river up the mountains he would never know.

With a huge sigh he kicked in another stone and turned back towards the bigtop. He wasn't going to get any answers looking at the river.

'I've got a puppet show to do so you can wait in the wagon,' Jac said as he skirted around the back of the stripped tent.

'But I'm a puppet, aren't I?' Dan looked

confused. 'Can't I come too?'

'Someone might see you,' Jac told him, worried what reactions he would get from a whole crowd of dwarves if they realised the puppet was alive.

'Did lady see I was real?' Dan argued.

'Lady? Oh Gabbi, no I guess she didn't. You're getting pretty good at being a lifeless puppet.' Jac had to agree.

'Then I can come,' Dan decided with the logic of a simple mind that could not be argued with. Jac changed direction again and headed for his small puppet theatre that he had put up a while ago.

There were dozens of small dwarf children crowded around the front of the theatre and Jac slipped into the covered back to set up his puppets. It was only a short show as the attention spans of the children, in both lands, was limited. He had five different stories and when they stayed in a town for any length of time he did five shows a day. He could do them in his sleep now as he'd been doing it since he was old enough to work the strings.

He drew the small curtain that marked the beginning of the show and the dwarf children jumped up and down in delight before being settled down by the parents who were milling around at the edges. They pretended they were there to watch the children but they laughed just as loud at the antics he put the puppets through.

Jac made Dan sit down at his feet as he began the show but within a few minutes Dan's own attention span had run out and he began to climb up the wooden framing that held up the material around the theatre. Jac couldn't do anything about it as he was in the middle of the show. Dan reached the mini-stage where Jac's puppets were chasing after a pig and he looked at the gathered children with wide-eyed surprise.

'Hello,' he said, and waved one wooden arm at them.

The children roared with laughter as his hand caught in the strings of one of the other puppets and the pig flew into the air. Dan grinned back at them and sank back out of sight. Throughout the rest of the show he kept popping his head up and waving, causing the children to laugh each time.

Just as the show was ending, Danel, who had come to see why the show was funnier than normal, climbed into the back with Jac. Danel grinned at Dan and they both popped their heads up onto the stage at the same time, causing an even bigger laugh just as the curtain came down.

Jac and Danel climbed out the back of the theatre, laughing, with Danel holding Dan. They didn't see Mr Blyne coming up from the back of the crowd of children who were all trying to find their parents at the same time. They didn't see him stand there, staring at them with great interest. But they did hear him yell.

'Jac! Danel! I want to see you at once in my wagon.' He marched off without waiting for them to acknowledge the summons and their laughter died instantly.

'Do you think he saw Dan?' Danel whispered as he tried to tuck the puppet under his arm. 'Should we leave him behind?'

'No, we can't leave him here and there's no time to take him to the wagon. He's good at staying still though. He'll be okay.' Jac tried to sound confident but he wasn't really. It would have been obvious to anyone who had seen the puppet show more than a couple of times that there had been no strings on Dan and Mr Blyne had seen the show more times than Jac could count.

They reached the red painted steps of Mr Blyne's wagon and hesitated, wanting to get it over with but not wanting to know what he wanted.

'Come in... hurry up.' Mr Blyne appeared at the top of the three steps but he was still not as tall as Jac. Jac tried to slouch so as not to make the ringmaster angry.

Jac and Danel went into the wagon and Jac immediately sat down cross-legged as he had been taught to, ever since he had grown taller than the ringmaster.

'I want to see that puppet,' Mr Blyne said as

soon as they were both inside and Jac's heart sank.

Danel was still holding him and he looked at Jac for permission to hand the little puppet over. Jac nodded briefly, knowing that there was no way to avoid it. Mr Blyne took Dan and looked critically at him. Thankfully Dan was playing dead and his arms swung limply as the ringmaster examined him.

'You made this?' He looked directly at Jac. 'And you can make them to look like anyone?'

'Yes, Mr Blyne,' Jac replied, amazed yet relieved, that he hadn't noticed Dan was real.

'And the strings?' Again he twisted Dan back and forth, looking for the non-existent strings.

'They're removable,' Danel chipped in, 'and so thin they can't be seen from a distance.'

'I want you to make two puppets for me,' Mr Blyne said in the nicest tone Jac had ever heard. He threw Dan to Jac and he caught him as softly as he could.

'Who do you want them to look like?' Jac asked, willing to agree to just about anything to get out of there fast.

'The bride and groom,' Mr Blyne stated, looking immensely pleased with himself. 'Such a wedding gift as that will make sure I get to do the entertainment.'

Jac had to hand it to Mr Blyne, he knew what

impressed people and this would certainly impress the king.

'I want those puppets in five days.' Mr Blyne had turned back to his demanding, blunt self as he dismissed them with a wave. 'And Marty's not well. You're filling in for him, Jac.'

Five days wasn't really a problem, unless Marty stayed sick for too long. It would be almost impossible to do five puppet shows and fill in as a clown twice a day as well as make the puppets.

Jac rushed off to put Dan in the wagon as there was no way he could take him into the bigtop while he was doing a show. Dan argued but eventually gave in when Jac promised to take him to look around the town as soon as he finished.

The first show at any town was always crowded and tonight was no exception. Jac saw the king in the red covered chair that had been placed ringside and Mr Blyne was working them harder than usual to impress the king. Tonight the ringmaster wore boots two inches lower than normal so that he was shorter than the king. Nobody in their right minds would insult King Jorth by making themselves taller than him. Dwarves were mistrustful by nature and even more so if someone was taller than them. Mr Blyne took care to keep the taller members of the troupe as far away as possible from the dwarf king.

Things went well through most of the show but towards the end things started to go wrong. Walking in the oversized shoes was hard enough but running was impossible. Jac lifted his knees as high as he could as tried to outrun the collapse of the burning building. It must have looked even more comical than it was supposed to as his bright red shoes slapped against the sawdust. Even with sweat pouring down his face Jac didn't let his over-painted smile slip. Mr Blyne would not tolerate that, ever.

The crowd roared with delight as the fake building missed him by only a few inches. No doubt they thought it part of the act but Jac knew it wasn't. It was supposed to burst into flames as he leapt from the window but it wasn't supposed to fall on him.

Pausing a second to catch his breath, Jac didn't see the other two clowns come up behind him. The first hint of trouble Jac had was another roar of the crowd then two buckets of water sent him flying forward to land face down on the arena floor.

Jac slowly pulled himself up, knowing by the silence of the crowd that their attention had been taken by another act. Otis and Mikal had refilled their buckets and were now dampening down the singed sawdust and the remains of the fake building.

'Sorry 'bout that Jac, we couldn't resist it.' Mikal was grinning as Jac stooped to help them clear the arena floor. The crowd was looking up at the high-wire act but Jac didn't even glance up at it. He had seen it thousands of times over the years and it no longer seemed exciting. The only job he hated worse than filling in for one of the clowns was up on the high wire with the trapeze a close second.

Not that he had much choice though; if someone was sick or injured he had to fill in. Sometimes being able to do all the circus acts wasn't as good as it sounded. He let the charred wood drop to the ground when they reached the backstage area and, slipping off the ill-fitting shoes, began to walk off. Mikal and Otis were busy arguing over how the building had collapsed. Neither of them was smiling now and the painted smiles looked out of place as they shouted and accused each other of sabotage. He hoped that Marty would be well enough to go on for the next show. Being a clown was a very hazardous occupation.

He left the bigtop and walked slowly across the long grass towards his wagon. The heavy flap of the huge red and white striped tent slapped back into place with a thud. The sounds of the performance were instantly dulled and after several more steps Jac could barely make out the crowd's applause. It was quiet out here with just a few birds chirping their disgust at the sun slipping behind the horizon and Jac shivered in his wet clothes. He would be expected to help clean up at the end of the show but Jac knew that Mr Blyne wouldn't notice his absence. He would be too busy making a beeline for the king.

Jac pulled his orange wig off and shook his shoulder length black hair free. He didn't care what anyone said, being a clown was a tough job. He arrived at his wagon and opened the door. Dan rushed out to meet him and Jac wondered what would have happened if it had been his mother. He still hadn't seen her since they arrived in Sweetwater but he wasn't in a hurry. He knew there was something big going on and that it involved him but he wasn't sure he wanted to know what it was.

'Jac gone long time. Dan lonely,' Dan said with a sad look on his face. 'Go out now?'

'I guess I did promise,' Jac agreed, knowing how important promises were to small children. 'Come on then.'

He stripped off his wet top and pulled on a dry shirt then picked Dan up and walked around the side of the bigtop towards the town. It would be almost empty while the show was still on and that suited Jac perfectly. He wasn't supposed to go into town because of his size and Mr Blyne would be furious if he found out.

Everything in Sweetwater was smaller than in the highlands. The street lamps were lower, so low that Jac had to duck under them, and even the trees seemed smaller. He crossed the small wooden bridge over the river that looked almost black in the half-light of dusk, wondering if it would hold his weight.

The streets were getting dark and at least one dwarf wasn't at the performance. He walked along the road on tall wooden stilts, making him almost as tall as Jac, with a lantern. He lit each street lamp as he went and Jac slipped behind one of the buildings to keep out sight until he passed by.

'You sure it's in Sweetwater?' a voice hissed as two men came into the alley in which Jac was hiding, blocking the only exit. Jac held a finger up to his mouth and Dan nodded in understanding.

'That's what he said, and I ain't goin' to argue with an archmage,' the other, taller man answered.

Jac saw the outline of the taller one as the dwarf on stilts lit a street lamp just outside the alleyway. It was Marty. So he wasn't sick after all and he seemed to know this archmage that Jac had been warned against.

'So where is it?' the smaller man let his voice

rise slightly and Jac was shocked to realise that it was Albot. He was more surprised that the elf and dwarf were working together than the fact that Albot was sneaking around in the dark planning something that was a bit suspicious.

'Up at the castle,' Marty replied. 'All we gotta do is go up there and find it.'

'I imagine it's guarded,' Albot pointed out and Jac almost laughed. It was just like Albot to be the cautious one when it was his own neck on the line.

'The map is worth the risk,' Marty assured him. 'And the Star Crystal.'

Star crystal. Map. That meant these were who had stolen Kimi's gems the other night. Jac wanted to go up and demand they returned them but that would give him away and he wanted to know more about the map and the Star Crystal.

'But don't you have to give the map to the archmage?' Albot sounded unsure at crossing this person.

'He never said we couldn't copy it. Then if we happen to get to the crystal before him that's his bad luck I reckon.' Marty laughed. 'We won't take the map until we're ready to leave town. No point in risking being found with it.'

The two conspirators walked out of the alley and Jac crept out after them. He watched them walk back towards the circus.

Who was this archmage who wanted both him and the Star Crystal? He didn't have anyone he could ask, except maybe Gabbi.

CHAPTER SIX
FLYING GUARDS

The streets were beginning to fill as Jac hurried back to the circus. He intended to go straight to Gabbi and find out what was going on. He was going to force her to tell him everything.

There was a new, small camp just off to the side of the circus and Jac crossed the rickety bridge slowly, trying to see who the two figures were that were silhouetted by the firelight. Was one of them that strange man on the horse, or maybe it was Marty and Albot?

It was neither and Jac frowned when he finally saw it was Gabbi and the old mime. He could tell they were deep in conversation by the closeness of their heads. Kimi was nowhere in sight so she must be in her cage and Jac wondered if anyone was watching her.

So how did Gabbi know the old mime? He had never come near the circus before, preferring to camp well away from everyone. For that matter, how could she have a conversation with someone who didn't speak? He moved further around behind them until he could see that the mime was indeed talking. He couldn't hear what the old man was saying but whatever it was Gabbi didn't seem to like it. She stood up; waving her arms angrily and the mime pulled her back down as if trying to convince her of something.

Suddenly the old man looked up, directly at Jac, a knowing look in his eyes that made Jac take several steps back in the dark. There was no way that the old man could see him, he was sure of that. Sitting so close to the bright fire would make the darkness impossible for the old man to see into, but his eyes followed Jac as he walked slowly around towards the circus camp.

Feeling very uneasy, Jac hurried back to his wagon. He decided that he wasn't really in a hurry to talk to Gabbi after all. Dan was fast asleep in his arms by the time he reached the wagon and he put the little puppet at the foot of his bed. His mother wasn't there, for which he was grateful as he wouldn't know what to say right now.

He lay on his bed, exhausted by the events of the day, and was asleep within seconds. He didn't really care if trolls were going to come and take him away or if this archmage was lurking outside the wagon, he was too tired to care.

Jac wasn't as upset the next morning to find he was hovering up near the roof. Dan was sitting happily on his chest, looking out the window, and he held the little puppet as he wondered how to control this floating. He consciously thought of his feet being on the floor and to his surprise he began to drift gently down.

Just to see what would happen, Jac thought about being up near the window and to Dan's delight they floated back up again. Once he was back with his feet firmly on the wagon floor Jac tapped his fingers on the wooden bedframe thoughtfully. If all he had to do was think about something and it happened then it could be disastrous. It bothered him that that was how Gabbi had described his magic and maybe that was all she meant, that he would have to be careful what he thought about.

'Jac, are you getting up this morning?' Zora's voice called through the thin curtain.

'I'm up,' Jac called back as he held one finger up to his lips and looked at Dan.

'I've brought breakfast in for you,' his mother said and Jac pulled back the curtain just enough to get through and then shut it again.

The small table had been folded down from the wall and a big breakfast for them both was on it. They hadn't eaten in their wagon in a long time and Jac's mind started imagining all kinds of reasons why she had done it today.

'I thought it might be nice to have a quiet meal, just the two of us like we used to do,' Madame Zora said as she loaded up her fork with a stack of food. One thing about living in a circus was that you never went hungry.

Jac sat down, feeling guilty that he had misread her intentions and they ate in silence. She didn't seem to be angry with him anymore and Jac relaxed as she smiled at him. Things seemed normal so far this morning, if you didn't count Dan and the floating. Hopefully nothing else would happen and their life would go on as it had before. There was no more talk of leaving the circus and Jac was reluctant to bring up any of the questions he had, for fear of breaking the happy mood his mother was in.

'I'll take the plates over,' Jac offered when they had finished their hearty meal. He gathered them up and was halfway out the door when he remembered Dan. Well, he would have to leave him there and hope he stayed quiet. On his way back Mr Blyne stopped him.

'Jac.' The ringmaster beamed at him, which Jac wasn't used to at all. He'd rather be treated with indifference like usual. 'How are the puppets coming?'

'The puppets?' Jac couldn't remember what he was talking about for a second and then it all came back to him. 'I haven't had time to start them yet since I was filling in for Marty.'

'Well, Marty is better today so you'll be able to get started, won't you?' Mr Blyne stuck his thumbs under the red braces that held up his striped trousers and inclined his head questioningly.

'I need wood...' Jac began.

'Then go and find some,' Mr Blyne countered.

'And to see what the bride and groom look like,' Jac finished and the ringmaster frowned.

'I suppose you do, at that,' he finally agreed after rubbing his chin thoughtfully for a full minute. 'Meet me at the front of the bigtop in half an hour. Bring that puppet and Danel as well.'

Jac didn't have a chance to ask why Danel and Dan had to come as the ringmaster turned and started bellowing at someone across the field. He rushed off to collect Dan and to find Danel, at least today was starting better than yesterday.

Jac didn't have a chance to tell Danel about the overheard conversation last night, nor Gabbi's outburst and her late night meeting with the old mime. By the time he had grabbed Dan, some paper, charcoal to draw with, and then found Danel rehearsing in the bigtop, they were late.

They ran around the tent and stopped abruptly as they almost ran into Albot and his father.

'Hurry along, we've a show to be back for in three hours,' Mr Blyne set off at a quick pace that Albot hurried to keep up with but Danel, being part elf, and Jac had no trouble with. The town was still waking up even though the circus had been awake for over an hour.

Jac trailed at the back, walking next to Danel

and carrying Dan. He ignored the curious stares of the dwarves who came to their doors and windows as he passed by. He never quite got used to it but he had learned to ignore it most of the time.

The houses were quite plain and small near the river but as they approached the castle gates they became bigger and fancier. The castle gates were huge, far bigger than they needed to be. Jac would have trouble climbing over so it would take three dwarves on top of each other to reach the top. They had been painted gold but here and there it was chipped and Jac could see the iron bars were rusting underneath.

Up ahead a long path led up to the castle, which sat on top of the only hill around for miles. Jac had never seen it up close before and he had to admit he was impressed. Dan let out a low whistle and Jac pretended it was him as Mr Blyne turned sharply to frown at him.

'Who comes?' A ferocious looking dwarf stepped in front of them. He was dressed in full battle armour and carried a spear that was far too long for him. Jac could see the dwarf could barely move under the weight of it all and he felt sorry for him.

'We must see King Jorth,' Mr Blyne announced calmly, obviously expecting the guard to step aside.

'Do you have an appointment?' The guard stood his ground and glared at them, with an extra long stare for Jac.

'The king will be happy to see us. We wish to discuss our gift for his daughter.' The ringmaster was not at all fazed by the guard and he puffed out his chest with self-importance.

'Very well,' the guard stood aside and lowered his spear. 'But the giant stays here.'

'That won't be possible. He is... an important part of the present,' Mr Blyne stated, seeming a little reluctant to admit that an elf had any importance at all.

'You're giving the princess a giant?' the guard almost laughed.

'Of course not,' Albot said in a sarcastic tone. 'Our gift is none of your business.'

The guard shrugged his shoulders and then leaned on one of the gates. He pushed as hard as he could and it only moved a few inches, sweat began to trickle down his face. Jac stepped forward and pushed the gate open easily and the guard glared at him.

'I can manage,' he stated nastily. 'I don't need help from a freak.'

'Suit yourself,' Jac said with a sigh and pulled the gate shut again.

The guard glared at him with pure hatred and heaved at the gate. Jac caught himself wondering what would happen if the guard couldn't open the gate. To his amusement the gate wouldn't budge, not even an inch. Mr Blyne stood impatiently tapping his foot while the guard heaved and puffed without success. Finally he called two other guards over and they too heaved and pushed but it didn't move.

It was with a shock that Jac realised his magic was holding the gate shut, because he was thinking it. He immediately stopped thinking about the gate staying shut and it swung open with such a force that the guards were thrown forward, landing face down on the cobbled path. Dan snickered quietly and Jac frowned. He was going to have to be careful what he thought from now on.

The ringmaster and his son stepped over the guards and marched up the path but Danel and Jac waited until the guards had moved away. The original guard avoided eye contact with Jac as he and his fellow guards started pushing the gate closed.

They were shown into a reception room at the front of the castle and Jac was told to sit on the floor at the back of the room. He would have sat on the floor anyway, as the chairs were so small that he would have been worried about them snapping under him. Even Danel looked out of place as he perched on the edge of the padded sofa.

'The king will see you now,' a houseguard, dressed in a stiff black jacket and white trousers came into the room and indicated that they should follow him. They were led down a wide corridor to another room, much like the first, where King Jorth sat on an immense throne. He wore a red velvet cape, trimmed with pure white fur, over a golden waistcoat and matching trousers. His crown sat lopsided on top of his overly wide head of golden curls. It was a spectacular sight but it was totally ruined by the sour expression on his face.

'Your Highness.' Mr Blyne and Albot bowed low and Albot kicked Jac and Danel in the ankle so they would follow suit. 'We come with the offer of a gift for the bride and groom.'

'And that is?' The king didn't beat about the bush and he looked from the ringmaster to Jac with an unpleasant frown.

'Jac. Sit!' Albot hissed and Jac had no option but to obey even though he felt like a puppy being taught a trick. He sank to the ground, cross-legged and the king returned his attention to Mr Blyne.

'Puppets, Your Highness,' Mr Blyne clicked his fingers and Albot snatched Dan from Jac's arms. Dan had been so still on the way up that Jac was worried he wouldn't be able to keep it up for much longer. Albot handed the puppet to his father who stepped forward and placed it in the king's hands.

'And why would I need a puppet?' The king was clearly unimpressed and barely looked at Dan.

'Danel.' Mr Blyne pulled him to the front of their little group and held out his hand for the puppet. He held Dan up next to Danel's face and pointed to the resemblance. 'We can offer one in the likeness of both bride and groom.'

'Really?' The king sounded more interested now and reached out for the puppet. This time he looked closer and Jac crossed his fingers that Dan would not blink. King Jorth smiled, and handed Dan back to Mr Blyne. 'That would be a suitable present. When will we receive it?'

'Our puppet master will need to make a drawing of the bride and groom,' Mr Blyne said with a grin from ear to ear as he pointed at Jac without turning around. 'Then the puppets will be ready in two days.'

Two days. Just yesterday he had five.

'Very well. Guard! Fetch Karlotte and Bradley.'

They were taken back to the first room and sat waiting patiently while Mr Blyne remained to discuss the entertainment at the wedding with King Jorth. After a few minutes a pretty, young dwarf girl came into the room by a side door just as an older lad, with immaculately tailored clothes, came in the double doors which led to the corridor.

'You wish to draw us?' the princess asked in a shy, pleasant voice as she sat on a twin-seated sofa and arranged her pretty, pink long dress around her feet. She pushed her long, well-tended blonde ringlets over her shoulder and placed her hands in her lap.

'Karlotte. Don't talk to commoners!' her groom-to-be snapped and she flinched at his words. 'Especially freaks like him.'

'But Bradley,' she protested but he waved a hand to silence her.

'Just hurry up freak,' Prince Bradley ordered and sat himself forcefully down on the seat next to his fiancée.

Jac bit his lip at the blunt and rude manner of the prince and got out his paper and charcoal. Danel took Dan over to look out the window and Albot wandered over to talk to the guard at the door.

The prince made no attempt to put his arm around the princess, or even speak to her, as Jac would have expected from a couple about to be married.

He made a rough sketch of Prince Bradley, knowing his face would be easy to remember anyway. It was an angry, sharp-featured face with thin lips and cruel eyes, all topped by black, and slicked-back short hair. He spent longer on Princess Karlotte's drawing, making sure he caught the gentleness and sweetness that was almost hidden by her obvious fear and dislike of her groom-to-be.

He glanced up at the door just as he put the finishing touches and raised an eyebrow at Albot discreetly handing a pile of gems to the guard who pocketed them immediately.

'I'll deliver it to you on the wedding day.'

Jac's excellent hearing only just caught the words and Albot nodded and moved away from the door.

Jac was willing to bet that Albot had just bribed the guard to steal the map. He turned back to his sketch before Albot could see him watching and added a last line to his drawing.

'That's long enough!' Prince Bradley stood up, pulling a reluctant Princess Karlotte after him. 'We have more pressing duties.'

He strode from the room with the princess following like a scared kitten just as Mr Blyne returned.

'We've done it!' he exclaimed, rubbing his hands with glee and then slapping Albot on the back. 'We're the entertainment at the wedding.'

'I can hardly wait for the day,' Albot said with a grin almost as wide as his father's but Jac knew that Albot had a different reason for looking forward to the wedding day.

CHAPTER SEVEN
BRING ME THE TALL ONE

There was only an hour before Jac's first show for the day and no time to waste. Now that he had only two days to make the puppets he needed the wood as soon as he could get it.

The groomer loaned him a horse and he rode off to the north where he knew of a small forest. It would be almost a half hour ride out there so he would not have much time to look for suitable wood. He spurred the horse on, not meaning to be unkind but desperate to get back in time and avoid Mr Blyne's bad temper.

'Faster. Faster,' Dan shouted, bouncing up and down happily as he clung to the saddle with his little wooden fingers. Jac did not dare leave him behind at the camp in case he was seen. Danel could not look after him as he had a new routine to learn that Mr Blyne had insisted be ready for the wedding show.

They made good time to the forest and Jac jumped down and tethered the horse to a tree. He began searching the forest floor for a suitable fallen limb and Dan clattered along after him. They had been searching for about ten minutes and Jac had just found one just big enough for both puppets' heads when they heard a loud boom.

'What was that?' Dan cried out as the noise echoed through the trees and shook the ground. He leapt up into Jac's arms and the bough fell to the ground.

'I don't know,' Jac admitted. The sound had come from somewhere up ahead and he went to see what had caused it.

'Dan go home.' The puppet's voice was a mere whisper and he was shaking but Jac could hear voices and he wanted to see who it was.

He stopped as the trees thinned out to form a small clearing and they both peered around a tree. What Jac saw made him regret being so inquisitive.

In the middle of the clearing stood a man and a group of six trolls. The man was the one who had ridden past them two days ago. And the trolls, who stood before the man, were the ones who attacked the camp. The man looked furious and there was a small patch of burnt grass in front of him but it didn't look as if there had been a campfire.

'What do you mean? If I say you will go into Sweetwater to fetch the boy... then you will. I'm sure of which one it is now so you only need to bring me the tall one,' the man boomed.

The tall one. That would be him! Jac shrank back behind the tree.

'But Archmage Ivan, Sir. Trolls are not permitted in Sweetwater. We will be locked up as soon as we are seen,' one of the trolls protested and Jac froze. This was the archmage? He peered around the tree again and looked at the man. He looked ordinary enough, if a little strange with his choice of clothes. What threat could this archmage be now that he had discovered his magic?

The answer came all too soon as the archmage pointed at the ground in front of the troll who had spoken and another boom rent the air. A second black spot appeared as the grass shrivelled in flames and the troll jumped back several steps.

'Then don't be seen,' he drawled.

The trolls backed away without further protest, thankfully in a different direction to where Jac had left the horse.

'Once I have the map it will only be a matter of time before I have the Star Crystal. And with the boy as well I will be the most powerful archmage in the world!' Ivan muttered to himself and then laughed. An evil sound made Jac shiver.

Jac began to back away, deciding he'd heard far more than he wanted to know. What in the lowlands did he have to do with the Star Crystal? But what bothered him most was what the sinister looking man could possibly want him.

'Dan go home?' Dan repeated in a tiny voice as they reached the fallen bough that Jac had dropped.

'Definitely,' Jac assured him, picking up the wood and heading back to the horse at a run. He wanted to get as far away from here as quickly as possible.

He rode as fast as the ageing horse would go and arrived back in town with only a few minutes to spare. The groomer was unimpressed at how hard he had ridden the horse but Jac had no time to stay and explain. For that matter, he wouldn't really know how to explain what had happened.

'Jac!' A bellow came from across the field and he stopped, recognising the ringmaster's voice. He wasn't that late, surely.

'Yes, Mr Blyne,' Jac answered as the little man hurried over to him. The ringmaster looked worried.

'The wedding...' he puffed and leaned his hands on his knees as he tried to catch his breath. 'It's been brought forward to tomorrow!' He finally caught his breath and pointed at the tree branch that Jac was holding. 'Haven't you started yet? They must be finished by tomorrow morning!'

'But that would take all day and most of the night,' Jac protested, even though he knew arguing was a waste of time.

'I'll get Albot to fill in for you at the puppet theatre. Just you get those puppets done on time or we'll all be in trouble.' Mr Blyne dismissed him with a shooing motion and went off, probably in search of his son. Jac knew Albot would not be pleased to be told to do the theatre and it was the only good thing about it all.

Jac stayed in his wagon for the rest of the day and carved the heads as quickly as he could. He took the bodies off two of the newest puppets as there wasn't time or enough wood to make arms and legs. For the groom he chose clothes that he had made for a mayor of a town they were due to visit soon and a puffy dress from a dancing puppet for the princess. He finally took a break as the evening show began and he pulled Danel aside.

'I'm on in ten minutes,' Danel reminded him.

'It won't take long,' Jac assured him as he led him to a quiet corner of the backstage area. He told him about Gabbi knowing about his magic, her late night meeting with the old mime, what he had overheard between Albot and Marty, and the people he'd seen in the forest today.

Danel looked understandably concerned by it all as he ignored his father's signal that it was time to get ready.

'What if they come for you tonight?' Danel waved his father off for a second time and frowned.

'I've thought of that,' Jac assured him. 'I'm going to spend the night in the last place any troll would ever look - with Kimi.'

'But Gabbi?' Danel started to argue but his father was starting to walk over towards them.

'Don't worry, she won't even know I'm there,' Jac assured his friend. 'I just wanted you to know what had been happening, just in case.'

Danel cast one final worried glance in his direction as he followed his father into the arena and then Jac slipped out of the tent. He went back to his wagon and collected Dan and the two almost finished puppets before heading for Kimi's wagon.

Kimi wasn't there, as she was waiting her turn to delight the crowd, and Jac climbed up on the roof for better light as the sun began to sink over the mountains. The moon would be almost full tonight so he would have enough light. If he kept at it the puppets should be finished by morning.

Dan sat next to him, happily watching the setting sun.

'Will they be real too?' Dan asked as the sun set and Jac stopped carving while he waited for the moon to rise. He hadn't brought a lantern as it would have given him away easily.

'Will what be real?' Jac replied, as he lay on his back to watch the stars appear one by one.

'The puppets, will they be real like me?' Dan had picked up the head of Princess Karlotte's puppet and smiled. 'She's pretty.'

'Real!' Jac sat bolt upright. It hadn't occurred to him that they might come alive like Dan had.

Jac frowned into the dark night as he tried to work out how he had made Dan real. It was just like everything else he'd done, he thought it.

'As long as I don't think about them being real we'll be fine.' Jac said, more confidently than he felt.

'You don't want them alive?' Dan sounded disappointed as he carefully laid the head back onto the roof of the wagon.

'I can't keep them anyway. If I was keeping them I would want them real, to be friends for you.' Jac tried to cheer the little puppet up

'Okay.' Dan seemed quite happy with that and Jac was relieved. There was no way he could keep three live puppets hidden.

Dan fell asleep as the moon came out and Jac went back to carving. He had left the drawings in his wagon, as he knew them without looking anymore. He was still working on the puppets when the show finished for the night and Gabbi put Kimi in her cage. Kimi rumbled a hello but didn't give away his presence on the roof. Jac finally finished and put the heads next to the thin wooden bodies. What if they did come alive? He pushed them to the far corner of the roof having decided to leave the heads off until tomorrow, just in case. He lay down and fell asleep instantly.

He was woken by whispering voices and he crawled to the edge of the roof to peer into the colourless night.

'I tell you I've searched every wagon. He's not here!' The voice hissed insistently.

'He has to be,' another said and Jac knew instantly that it was the trolls. If he stayed quiet they'd never find him up here.

'We can't go back without him again,' a third said with fear in his voice.

Kimi stirred and rumbled in her sleep making the trolls hastily move further away from her cage. Jac watched as the trolls moved back along the wagons, peering into each one before they finally disappeared into the darkness. He lay listening for what seemed like hours, in case they came back, but heard nothing and finally nodded back off to sleep.

'It's morning Jac,' a deep rumble from under the roof woke him and he opened his eyes reluctantly. 'Gabbi has gone to look for you.'

'Thanks Kimi,' Jac leaned his head over the edge and rubbed the ridge above her eyes. 'Time to leave I guess.'

He gathered up the sleeping Dan and put all the puppet parts of the two royals in a sack he had brought. He jumped down, landing lightly, and headed off to his wagon.

There was something going on around the front of the bigtop and Jac detoured to see what it was. There were dwarves running everywhere, angry dwarves and several dozen guards, shouting orders. The wagons and tents of the dwarf troupe who had arrived the day before them were being moved.

'The wedding marquee will go here,' one guard shouted, barely heard above all the others. 'Move along. Move along.'

The dwarves did not look happy at being moved further down the town to a smaller field that was well away from today's events. Jac watched for a minute while a huge tent began to be put up and he wondered why the wedding was today as the planned date was still weeks away.

'Jac, where are the puppets?' Mr Blyne came around the tent and caught Jac by surprise. Dan flinched as he woke up and Jac held him behind his back.

'In here,' Jac held up the sack and to his horror Mr Blyne snatched it from him. 'But the heads aren't attached yet.'

'I've not been a ringmaster for thirty years without knowing how to put a head on a puppet.' He opened the sack and pulled out the wooden princess' head and nodded, satisfied with what he saw. He put it back and took the other one out, and then his smile disappeared. 'This doesn't look like right!'

'It doesn't?' Jac asked, surprised. He looked closer at the wooden head but couldn't see anything wrong with it. 'Looks okay to me.'

'It makes him look angry and cruel.' The ringmaster jumped up and down angrily.

'Well, that's how he looked when he sat for the drawing.' Jac defended himself.

'It'll have to do. If the king doesn't like it I'll make your life so miserable you'll wish you were never born!' Mr Blyne almost threw the head back into the sack and stormed off.

Jac brought Dan from behind his back, thankful that he had kept quiet.

'Here comes Gabbi,' Dan informed him and pointed over his shoulder.

Jac ducked under the heavy canvas tent and ran across the arena to the other side. He came out the back and went around to the far end of the field. He wasn't in the mood for Gabbi right now.

Huge black clouds started floating in from every direction and a minute later spots of rain began to fall. Winter storms here were known for their suddenness and ferocity. Jac looked around for Gabbi and ran for cover. He had almost reached his wagon when, from underneath it, came six trolls. They glared at him and started walking towards him. Their heavy woollen clothes were covered in dirt from hiding under the wagon and the smears of mud on their faces made them look even more fearsome.

'I told you he'd have to come back eventually,' the biggest troll said to the others.

Jac began to back away towards the river as he tried to see how he was going to get out of this. The determined look on the trolls' faces said they weren't going to give up easily this time. The freezing cold rain was pelting down now and Jac was soaked to the skin.

'Dan go home,' Dan whispered, and before Jac could stop him the little puppet had jumped down and run off.

'What was that?' One of them asked suspiciously.

'Just get the boy!' the biggest troll said as he gave the other one a shove forward.

They were only a few steps from him now and Jac wondered if he should jump in the river. He glanced at it and decided it was safer to face the trolls.

'The archmage will be pleased with us this time,' the biggest one muttered and that gave Jac an idea.

He raised his arm as he had seen Ivan do and pointed at the ground in front of the trolls, thinking of a black patch of grass.

He was almost as shocked as the trolls when it actually worked and a black circle appeared on the grass along with a boom of sound. Jac frowned as it didn't look quite the same though. This was a hole, not just some charred grass. Smoke hissed from the hole as rain continued to pour from the sky and after one brief look into it the trolls looked at each other.

'I'm not taking him on,' one said, turning and running. The others quickly followed him, and Jac breathed a sigh of relief. He had just allowed himself a small smile of satisfaction when he noticed he was being watched.

Madame Zora, Gabbi, and the old mime stood about ten feet away. All of them looked angry, and Gabbi was holding a squirming Dan.

CHAPTER EIGHT
THE HOLE

'Jac!' His mother bellowed, her voice carrying easily to him despite the torrential rain. 'What have you done?'

Jac stepped around the smoking hole, he wasn't sure if it was smoke or mist from the rain but it wasn't good, and walked towards the trio. They turned and walked off as he reached them and he followed them over to his wagon.

'I think we'd better talk in there.' The mime spoke clearly and with such authority that nobody argued, least of all Jac. He knew he was in the biggest trouble of his life and he steeled himself against what was to come.

Usually Madame Zora would have rushed about getting towels to stop the water dripping on the worn red rug inside their wagon but she just stood there, glaring at him, while puddles formed around their feet.

Gabbi paused at the door, handed Dan to Madame Zora, then leaned back out and called softly.

'Kimi.'

Within seconds, Kimi back-winged gently down next to the wagon. 'Stay here. Don't let anyone in.'

'He meant no harm,' Kimi spoke in her low, rumbling voice that was easily heard inside the wagon.

From the angle he was on, Jac could only see one side of Gabbi's face but the colour had drained from it as she stared out at her dragon.

'You knew what he was!' Gabbi stepped out into the pouring rain and looked up at Kimi.

'I knew who he was. He needed a friend to watch over him,' came the quick reply.

'Surely you knew we searched for ones like him.' It was a statement rather than a question.

'But you wished to harm him. I did not,' Kimi replied simply.

'Harm him? No, we wanted to protect him... from himself,' Gabbi stammered back, defensive and angry now.

The mime had joined her outside and Jac watched with his mother who was still holding Dan. Gabbi wanted to hurt him? Surely not. Kimi must be mistaken.

'By taking away his magic and keeping his mind forever like a child's? How does this not harm him?' Scorn crept into Kimi's voice and a small flame shot from her nostril, despite the rain that continued to fall.

'It is for his own good. We have done it to many children in the past.' The mime stepped forward but Kimi flared her nostrils and hissed so he stepped back again.

'And kept them from ever living to experience life as they should! You destroy a great mind, a great person, for what?' Kimi almost bellowed and the mime looked quickly around to see if anyone was close enough to listen. The area was deserted though, because of the rain, and he turned back to Kimi.

'It is for the best,' the mime said, a little less angry and with a tinge of regret in his voice.

Kimi fell silent but her glare spoke for her. Who's best? She turned her back on Gabbi and the old mime and sat, on guard, as she had been instructed.

Jac realised that his mouth had dropped open and he closed it as the shock began to pass. Could they really take away his magic and turn his mind into that of a child? Would they do it to him now? Perhaps he could still make a run for it. He looked over at the window, seeing that it was open and the rain was driving in fiercely. He might just have time to grab Dan and make a dash for it.

'Don't worry, I won't let them.' His mother spoke softly and he turned to look at her with a sigh of relief.

'Fine by me,' Jac muttered, taking a step back as Gabbi and the old mime were coming back inside, looking grim and worried.

'Why did you do it?' The mime looked more sad than angry and he waved his hands expressively and pointing at Dan, who sat shivering in Madame Zora's arms.

'I didn't mean to. How was I supposed to know Dan would become real?' Jac replied defensively and reached over to take the puppet. He held Dan comfortingly and turned him away from the angry stares that were directed at him. 'Anyway, he's just a little puppet. He can't do any harm.'

'Dan frightened,' Dan whispered as he tried to snuggle deep into Jac's soaked clothes.

'Yes, he's just a puppet, but what will you do next?' The mime turned his attention to Madame Zora. 'Didn't you warn him that his magic could destroy us all?'

'There was no need. I had him believing that magic was nonsense ever since he was a tiny boy. Besides I held a dampening spell over him to stop his magic from developing.' She sighed, a heavy and regretful sound that made Jac want to put his arm around her and comfort her too. 'But his magic was too strong.'

'You can do magic?' Jac was more surprised by that than anything else he'd heard so far today. How could he have lived with her his whole life without knowing?

'She's an archmage, like my grandfather, Trel, and I'm a mage,' Gabbi told him, pointing at the mime and then she glared at Mme Zora. 'You hid it well.

'Then I'm a mage too?' Jac decided it was time they answered some of his questions. 'So why is my magic so bad when yours isn't?'

'Jac's magic not bad. Jac make Dan,' Dan stated defensively.

'Yes you are a mage, Jac,' his mother said, coming over to take him by the arm gently. She looked at him with sad, regretful eyes that made him wonder what sort of bad news she was about to give him. 'But your magic is too strong. You can do things that even you cannot imagine.'

'That doesn't sound so bad,' Jac said, feeling confused.

'All elves are born with some magic within them. Most never even realise it but some are strong enough to come to our attention,' Trel said with a sigh as he sank down in to a chair, dripping water everywhere.

'What do you do with them?' Jac asked suspiciously.

'Do?' Trel looked confused. 'We train them to use their magic and they become mages. When their magic is strong enough they become archmages.'

'So why can't you train me to use mine?' Jac didn't direct his question at just Trel and all three of them looked uncomfortable.

'We don't know how to use magic as strong as yours. It doesn't seem to follow the rules that apply to our own magic. We simply don't know how to control it,' his mother answered sadly.

'So you just take it away because you don't understand it?' Jac replied with a hint of bitterness in his voice.

'I tried to hide it from you, not take it away,' his mother explained.

'And Archmage Ivan, what does he want from me?' Jac knew there was no way he was going to let anyone take away anything from him.

'You know him?' Trel looked worried, surprised and very suspicious.

'Those trolls were supposed to take me to him,' Jac explained. 'But I don't actually know him. I saw him in the forest yesterday when I went for wood. That's where I saw that pointing at the ground trick.'

'He's evil,' Gabbi said with an expression as if she had just tasted something sour and spat it out.

'And he wants to take my magic too?' Jac asked defiantly. What right did any of them have to keep it from him?

'Sort of, 'his mother replied. 'Not everyone thought the answer was to stop the minds of the gifted ones from ever growing up. I used to, until you… were born.' Zora paused.

Her mind seemed to wander somewhere far off. A look of deep regret and sorrow passed over her face, and then she continued.

'I managed to save you but...' Again she paused and Jac could tell there was something she wasn't telling them. 'I thought that I could suppress your magic and eventually it would go away, and then there would be no more problems. It seems I was wrong.' She sighed and cast a sidelong glance at Gabbi and Trel.

'Each gifted child's magic is locked within the Star Crystal and Ivan believes that if he can get hold of it, and a gifted one, he will be able to transfer it all to himself. That would give him enough power to rule everyone and everything around him.'

'Can he?' Jac asked uneasily. No wonder Ivan wanted him so badly.

'We don't know,' Zora answered. 'But we do know that we can only channel magic one way... into the Star Crystal. Perhaps a gifted one, like you, could bring it back out again.'

'We need to get hold of the Star Crystal before Ivan does. It's too powerful to be in his hands.' Trel rubbed his soggy beard thoughtfully, a deep frown creasing his forehead.

'Where is it?' Jac asked. If they were going to try to put his magic inside it, then the further away it was, the better.

'Ivan tried to steal it many times so we had to use our magic to hide it,' Trel explained. 'We cast it to the winds, high on Mt Vane, and created a map that could lead us to it when we needed it.'

'But the map was stolen over a year ago,' Gabbi added.

'And without this Star Crystal you can't take my magic away,' Jac stated. He decided that he would get hold of the crystal himself to stop them taking his or anyone else's magic.

'Without the map they will never find it,' Zora informed him.

'Star crystal… Map…' Jac muttered to himself, realising that his fate was more entwined with it all than he had imagined. 'Albot!'

'What about Albot?' Three surprised faces turned to him and they spoke as one.

'He's getting the map today sometime,' Jac told them reluctantly. He didn't want them finding the crystal and he could have kicked himself for speaking without thinking first.

Zora's eyebrows rose a full inch. 'Where is he getting it from?'

'I overheard him bribe a houseguard at the castle yesterday so I guess the king has it,' Jac replied with a shrug. 'He and Marty are supposed to deliver it to Ivan.'

'Hey Jac!' Danel's voice came from just outside and then the door opened. 'Jac are you okay?'

Danel paused at the doorway, drenched from the rain, as he looked at the assembled group with a cautious glance.

'Kimi, you were supposed to stop him,' Gabbi called out the door.

'He already knows,' Kimi rumbled. 'He is Jac's friend.'

'You told them about Dan?' Danel asked with a wry smile at the little puppet.

'I'll tell you about it later,' Jac promised him and got an angry look from all three gathered there.

'He doesn't need to know!' Trel ordered. 'The less who are involved the better.'

'He's already involved,' Jac retorted. 'And he's the only one who hasn't yelled at me so far, except for Kimi.'

'What's with the hole outside? I almost stepped in it.' Danel pointed out the window. The rain had eased off now to a light drizzle and Jac could see the hole over near the river. Something didn't seem right though. It looked different.

'Where are you going?' Gabbi snapped at Jac as he walked to the still open door.

'I need to see something.' He decided he wasn't going to let her push him around. He walked over to the hole, followed by Danel and Kimi.

'It grows,' Kimi stated and Jac gulped in horror. The small hole he had made was growing, very slowly, but it was inching its way outward. He watched, transfixed, as it crept towards the river. Gabbi, Trel and Zora had joined them by the time the hole reached the edge of the murky water.

Jac held his breath as the water began to spill over the edge and pour into it. How big was it going to get?

'I can't hear it,' Danel said, leaning dangerously close to the edge.

'Hear what?' Jac asked, stepping back and pulling Danel to a safe distance.

'The water. I can't hear it hitting the bottom.'

Jac leaned closer and listened. The water kept pouring in but Danel was right, he couldn't hear anything else. Just how deep was it?

'Jac! Jac!' A desperate, angry and frightened cry came from behind them and he spun, almost falling into the hole, to see who wanted him now. Mr Blyne was hurrying across the sodden ground, looking like he had just seen someone stealing all his treasure. He was carrying a sack and Jac recognised it as the one he had put the two puppets into. Didn't the king like them?

It was a second later that Jac knew it wasn't that simple. An angry king would be nothing compared to the real problem. The sack was moving as if something inside was struggling to get out.

CHAPTER NINE
MORE PUPPETS

'What's in the sack?' Zora leaned down to ask him in a quiet voice as the ringmaster hurried towards them.

'More puppets,' Jac replied with a heavy sigh. 'They look like the princess and her intended.'

'Didn't you learn anything after seeing that one come alive?' Gabbi hissed at him and pointed angrily at Dan. She made a waving motion at Kimi and she flew off, probably back to her wagon.

'I didn't know it would happen again.' Jac attempted to defend himself but even to him it sounded a weak defence.

'Jac, what is the meaning of this!' Mr Blyne had reached them and, without actually thinking about it, they all lined up to hide the hole.

'Of what?' Jac put on an innocent face and held Dan behind his back.

'These puppets. They move and talk!' he exploded and shook the sack under Jac's nose.

'Really?' Zora stepped forward and took the sack from him. She opened the top and peered in for a brief second before shrugging her shoulders and handing it back to the ringmaster. 'They don't seem to be moving to me.'

'They don't?' Mr Blyne dropped the sack to the ground and peeled down the sides to expose the two puppets.

Jac held his breath, wondering what his mother had done. The puppets just lay in a heap just as any other wooden puppet would do and did not appear to be alive at all.

'But I saw them move. They talked to me!' Mr Blyne shook his head in confusion and disbelief.

'I think you've had too much sun,' Zora said comfortingly and pulled the sack closed before putting it into the hands of the bemused ringmaster.

'Sun?' Mr Blyne looked up into the slowly falling drizzle.

'Don't you need to deliver the present?' Jac asked and the ringmaster stared at him with eyes that didn't quite focus.

'Present? Oh yes, must deliver the present.' He turned and wandered off slowly as the rain trickled to a stop.

'What did you do?' Jac asked as he stepped forward to avoid the still growing hole. He turned to look at it with a growing sense of unease and saw the river was still pouring into it. There was very little water getting past it and the riverbed further down was drying up fast, soon there would be no water through the whole town. Eventually someone would come to look why there was no water to turn the wheels of their mills. 'How did you turn them back into just puppets?'

'Back into puppets?' Dan cried out as Jac brought him from behind his back again. 'Want friends!'

'I didn't turn them back into puppets,' Zora told him. Dan looked delighted but Jac frowned, not understanding. 'I simply switched them for lifeless puppets. The real ones are in the wagon.'

'Great!' Dan wriggled free and bounded off towards the wagon, clicking and clacking loudly, with a delighted grin on his wooden face.

'Are there any more you haven't told us about?' Trel asked bluntly as he indicated that they too should go back to the wagon.

'No,' Jac replied quietly. He should have refused to make them as soon as Dan asked if they would be real. He should have known better.

'Don't sweat it Jac,' Danel came up next to him and slapped him on the back in a friendly gesture. 'At least Dan has some company now. And how did your mother switch them? I didn't see it.'

'There are a few things you don't know,' Jac said with a heavy sigh. 'My mother can do magic, she's an archmage, and so is Gabbi's grandfather.'

'Really? Danel raised both eyebrows in surprise but his step did not falter. 'A few days ago I don't think I would have believed you but what with that hole, Dan, and those trolls after you, I would believe just about anything now.'

'Good, because there's more but I'll tell you later.' Jac fell silent as he reached the open door to his wagon. The sun peeked out of a gap in the clouds and steam was beginning to rise from the ground as the rain evaporated.

Everyone crowded into the wagon and stood in a circle around the sack, which sat in the middle of the floor. Dan had arrived first and he was busy trying to free the two wriggling puppets from the sack.

'Let me out of here!' A bellow came from within the sack.

Dan pulled the sides down and just as he freed the two puppets he fell backwards, having been punched squarely in the nose by one of them.

'How dare you put me in a sack?'

Dan sat up, rubbing his nose and stared at the little puppet who had struck him. It was the one carved in the likeness of Bradley and he didn't look happy. His face was set in a very unfriendly expression, even more so than the one Jac had carved and his temper seemed well matched to it.

'If you put me in there again I'll have you whipped!' he exploded as he stamped his foot and glared at Dan again.

All of a sudden the new puppet noticed that there were others in the wagon, and that they were all much, much bigger than him. He turned in a circle, took one nervous step backwards, bumped into Dan, whirled on him and punched him on the chin. Dan fell to the floor again and got up looking confused but unhurt.

'Why do you keep doing that?' Dan asked but the puppet just glared at him.

'Brad's just mean,' a quiet voice came from the folds of the sack and Jac saw the little Karlotte peering cautiously out.

'You can keep quiet, Lotte.' Brad rounded on her and Zora stepped in before he reached the little puppet.

'That's quite enough out of you now,' she said firmly as she scooped him up and pinned his arms to his sides with one hand. Brad wriggled furiously and then tried to bite her but she ignored him. Jac decided that Brad was even more bad tempered than the real Bradley.

'We won't hurt you.' Jac sat cross-legged as he urged Lotte out of the sack. She came out slowly, looking to make sure that Brad wasn't going to get free.

'Hi, I'm Dan.' Dan rushed in front of her, blocking Jac's view.

'I'm Lotte. Where am I?' she asked Dan.

There was a lot of noise coming from just outside the wagon and everyone, except Jac, went to look out of the window.

'It's the king's guards,' Trel muttered.

'You can look after Lotte,' Jac told Dan as he picked the two of them up and placed them on his bed before pulling the curtain to hide them. 'If anyone comes in you can teach her that little game we play.'

Jac went to join the others and saw Zora putting a limp Brad into the sack.

'He's just asleep. He'll sleep for quite a few hours,' she explained when he raised an eyebrow in surprise. She tied a knot in the sack and hung it from a hook on the wall. 'Don't worry he won't suffocate, there are holes in the sack.'

Jac felt a little guilty that he hadn't even thought about that. He didn't like the little puppet at all and felt absolutely no sympathy for him being put back into the sack. Jac followed the others, including Zora, outside. The king's guards were moving along the row of wagons, searching them and yelling to each other as they did.

'This one's been done. No sign here,' one yelled to his fellow guard and they moved on to the next wagon. 'Everybody out!'

'They must be looking for the map,' Gabbi whispered. 'I think it's time we paid Albot a visit.'

'I'll come with you,' Trel stated and the two of them hurried off towards Albot's wagon.

'Is this the map you were talking about yesterday?' Danel asked and Jac nodded.

'We need it,' Jac said a little distantly. What would the king's guards think when they saw the huge hole that was spreading across the field and swallowing up the river?

'I saw Albot and Marty heading up past the bigtop when I was coming here,' Danel said and Zora frowned.

'You two had better go up that way and see if you can find them,' she said and as Jac was about to protest about leaving the puppets and the hole she continued. 'I'll try to stop the hole getting any bigger and I'll take the puppets with me.'

Having no reason to argue, Jac and Danel turned to leave just as the king's guards reached the wagon next to them. They had to find that map before the guards did.

The ground underfoot was drying out fast and there were only a few puddles left by the time they had gone around the bigtop and arrived at the huge wedding marquee. It looked like the rain would not put off the wedding at all. Dwarves were running around setting up seats and flowers, ignoring Jac and Danel as they looked around for any sign of Albot or Marty.

They moved on across the field, looking down between wagons and behind tents until they reached the bridge that led into town. There was no sign of them anywhere and they stood on the bridge, wondering what to do next. The water in the river had been reduced to a small trickle so obviously Zora hadn't found a way to stop the hole growing yet.

'I feel like a troll,' a muttered voice came from beneath their feet.

Jac held one finger up to his lips and they stood perfectly still and listened.

'Nobody will think to look for us under here,' replied another voice. Jac mouthed the word 'Marty' and Danel nodded.

'Where's all the water gone?' Albot's voice drifted up through the thin wood.

'Who cares, it stunk anyway.'

A king's guard was walking in their direction and Jac pulled Danel quietly off the bridge and into a small clump of bushes nearby. The guard appeared to be heading straight for the bridge and at the last minute he turned to look nervously around and then slipped quickly down the bank.

'You took your time!' Albot hissed. 'Have you got it?'

'Of course I have,' the guard snapped in reply. 'Where are the rest of my gems?'

A faint clinking told of the exchange and then there was a brief silence.

'That's it?' Marty didn't sound convinced. 'I thought it would be bigger.'

'Do you want it or not?' the guard demanded. 'You wouldn't have got it at all if I didn't have the perfect excuse to come down here. With everything else he's got to worry about the king won't even notice it has gone for a few days at the least. For that matter he doesn't have a clue what it is for. He only bought it off the traveller because he thought it was unusual. So, do you want it?'

'We want it,' Albot assured the guard and then there were some more clinks. 'Here's a few more for your trouble.'

'I'd better get back and join the search before my captain notices I'm missing,' the guard said and a few seconds later he appeared at the top of the bank. Jac saw him look back down at the river, frowning, and then hurried off back towards the circus.

Jac and Danel watched and waited for a few more minutes but neither Albot nor Marty came out from under the bridge. Jac had no idea what they could be doing under there but there might be just enough time to go and get some help. He doubted if they would give up the map willingly.

Something bothered him though and he told

Danel as they dashed back towards Zora and the hole.

'If they don't know the map is missing yet, what are they searching the circus for?' he asked and Danel shrugged.

'I've no idea; perhaps something else has been stolen?' Danel suggested as he turned back to look at the bridge. 'Look!'

Jac stopped and almost swore when he saw Marty jump onto a horse that must have been under the bridge with them and then ride off out of town. Albot was walking up the hill, whistling happily, with his hands in his pockets, looking as if he had just found hidden treasure.

'Quick we've got to get horses and follow him. If he reaches Ivan we're in trouble.' Jac pulled Danel after him as he hurried off.

'Wouldn't Kimi be faster than a horse?' Danel asked and Jac grinned.

'Great idea.'

They had just reached Kimi's wagon when Gabbi arrived, looking very worried.

'He's not in his wagon and we can't find him anywhere.'

'Marty's got the map. He's ridden off out of town,' Danel told her and she looked at Jac for confirmation.

'He's got a big head start,' Jac added and looked up at Kimi, lying sleepily on the roof.

'Any chance of Kimi taking us to catch him?' Danel asked boldly.

'Of course,' Kimi rumbled before Gabbi could answer and she lifted gracefully off the roof, settling next to them and lowering one wing. 'But I can only carry two.'

'I guess that means I stay here,' Danel said with a sigh.

'Go and tell the others where we're going,' Gabbi told him as she jumped easily up onto Kimi's back.

Jac climbed up too, unsure where he should sit and wishing he'd never let Danel suggest the idea. There didn't seem to be anything to hold on to. For all his dreams of flying on Kimi, he'd never really wanted to do it for real. He hated heights!

'Hurry up Jac,' Gabbi snapped.

He sat down behind her and reluctantly grabbed hold of her waist as Kimi lifted suddenly into the air. It was nothing like in his dreams as the world below him shrank at an alarming speed and his stomach lurched as Kimi caught an air current and rose even quicker.

'Which way?' Gabbi called back to him.

'That way.' Jac pointed as he forced himself not to shut his eyes. The forest didn't look very far away from up here but it looked very small. He gripped as tight as his legs could when Kimi leaned to turn into a graceful dive. It didn't feel graceful with the wind whipping his hair painfully about his face and bugs hitting him every few seconds.

'There he is.' Gabbi jabbed him with her elbow and he realised he was holding her too tightly.

He looked down, instantly regretting it as his head began to swim, and saw a horse almost at the trees. Kimi pulled her wings back and Jac felt the colour drain from his face as she went into a nosedive, straight at Marty.

CHAPTER TEN
A COPY WON'T DO

Jac didn't feel the landing as he was too busy trying to stay on Kimi's back and it wasn't until Gabbi started to climb off that he realised they were on the ground. He slid off and heaved a huge sigh of relief when his feet touched the ground. If he never flew again it would be fine with him.

'There's his horse.' Gabbi, not noticing Jac's relief at being safely on the ground, pointed over to a horse that was tethered to a small tree by the edge of the woods. Marty was nowhere in sight though. 'We'll have to go after him on foot. We wouldn't be able to see much through the trees from on Kimi's back. Besides I don't want Kimi anywhere near Ivan.'

'That's fine by me,' Jac muttered as he started walking towards the trees. His legs felt like rubber but he kept going. Marty didn't have much of a head start so they should catch up with him easily. He wondered why Gabbi wanted Kimi kept away from Ivan but he didn't think it was the time to ask. 'I think I know where he's heading.'

Jac led Gabbi quickly through the forest. He began to wonder just what they were going to do when they caught up with him and he hoped that Gabbi had a plan. Jac held out a hand to slow Gabbi down just as they came near to the clearing he had seen Ivan in.

'They were just up ahead yesterday,' Jac whispered. It felt like much more than a day had past since he had last been here. So much had happened in such a short space of time.

Jac and Gabbi crept closer until they could see into the clearing. Sure enough Marty was standing in the middle, but he was alone. There was no sign of Ivan and only the charred circles of grass told Jac that this was indeed the same clearing. He began to wonder if Zora had found a way to stop the hole from growing yet but his thoughts were interrupted by a gasp of shock from Marty.

'What was that?' Jac hissed and Gabbi held a finger to her lips. A large area of smoke appeared in the centre of the clearing and Marty took several steps backwards.

'It's a travelling spell,' Gabbi whispered back, so quietly that Jac barely heard her. 'It only lasts a short while though and then you go back to where you started from.'

'So he's not really living in the woods?' Jac muttered, wondering why he had ever thought such a powerful archmage would live rough in a forest.

'You have the map?' Ivan rasped, looking eager and excited, as the smoke faded away.

'I do,' Marty said coolly and waved his small satchel that was slung over his shoulder. 'But I want payment first.'

'Payment!' Ivan laughed and it was a loud, rock crunching sound. 'Let's just say your life is payment enough.'

Ivan's body seemed to grow taller and Marty took another step back. Soon he would be within an arm's stretch of Jac and Gabbi.

'It's just an illusion,' Gabbi whispered to Jac.

'It's a good one,' Jac commented. He wouldn't have stood his ground either.

'I… I guess that's a pretty good deal,' Marty stammered as he took off the satchel and threw it to the ground just in front of Ivan.

Jac pulled himself free from Gabbi and dashed out into the clearing.

'Jac!' Gabbi hissed but he didn't stop. If he didn't get the map soon it would be out of their reach completely. He ran past a very surprised Marty, snatched up the satchel from in front of Ivan and ran for the trees as quickly as he could.

'Ah. You have come to me.' Ivan stared after Jac, who couldn't help but turn to look at him as he reached the cover of the trees. He knew he should be running for his life but somehow he felt drawn to him.

'Bring it here, boy,' Ivan said in a compelling voice that tugged strangely at Jac. Without meaning to, Jac found himself walking slowly towards the archmage.

'Jac! No!' Gabbi burst from the bushes and Marty, finally gathering his wits about him, dashed off into the trees in the direction of his horse.

'Gabbi, so nice of you to visit.' Ivan didn't look at all surprised to see her and he glanced up at the sky that was just visible through the small gap in the trees. 'And where is your dragon?'

'She's safe. Away from you,' Gabbi hissed.

'I would never hurt your dragon.' Ivan tried to look innocent but it didn't reach his eyes. 'I'm sure she would be happier in my care.'

'Just like the one you had before who you pushed so hard that he fell to his death, too exhausted to fly?' Gabbi retorted angrily.

Jac fought the need to go to Ivan and found he could move on his own again. Ivan saw Jac was no long in his control and looked surprised.

'You can fight me at such a young age?' Ivan looked a little unsure of himself as his face settled into a firm concentrated stare and he began to mumble angrily.

Again Jac felt the desire to go to Ivan wash over him but he banished it with a flick of his hand and stared back at Ivan defiantly.

'You will never control me,' Jac declared as he clung to the satchel. 'And you will never have the map.'

For a brief few seconds Ivan looked angry, and then he smiled. A leering, calculated smile made Jac uncomfortable.

'Join me, boy. Together there's no limit to the things we could do,' Ivan suggested softly. 'Why let the likes of Gabbi and Trel tell you what to do? With the Star Crystal we could rule the world!'

'I don't want to rule the world,' Jac stated firmly and coldly. He stared at the ground in front of Ivan where the two circles of burnt grass still showed clearly. He wished he could have done one like that back in Sweetwater instead of that rotten hole. After all, it was just singed grass.

'Come with me, boy, or I will force you to!' Ivan demanded. 'I am the strongest archmage ever born. Nobody defies me!'

'No," Jac replied angrily. He had had enough of people telling him what to do and without thinking about it he raised his arm and shook it angrily.

'Jac, don't! Remember what happened before,' Gabbi cried out in alarm but it was too late.

A loud boom echoed through the forest as a perfect circle of black, singed grass appeared right at Ivan's feet. Ivan jumped back hastily and shot a look of frustrated anger at Jac, obviously realising that he was too strong an opponent after all.

Jac looked at the circle in surprise. He felt a small amount of pride and a large amount of relief as it could so easily have been another hole.

Ivan took several steps toward Gabbi. He grabbed her as his illusion of huge size disappeared and then turned to Jac. Gabbi struggled but Ivan hit her hard across the face and she hung limp in his arms with her eyes closed.

'How about we make a deal?' Ivan drawled, looking smug. 'If you come with me willingly, and bring the map, I'll let her go. If not…'

Jac gulped. What would Ivan do to Gabbi? He stared at Ivan for several seconds before he had an idea. He pulled open the satchel and looked at the parchment inside. It was a simple map and much smaller than he expected as it was just a few lines and symbols. Obviously it would mean something to Trel or Zora but it meant nothing to him. He looked at it one more time, committing the lines and marks to memory. It was something he was good at and he knew he would have no trouble making a copy of it later. All they had to do was beat him to the Star Crystal.

He closed the satchel and with a quick flick of

his wrist he flung it in the air, high above Ivan.

'Catch!' he called.

Ivan dropped Gabbi to the ground as he stretched for the satchel. He had just grabbed hold of it when the smoke returned, engulfing them all. It wasn't like the smoke from a fire, more like a mist on a lake in the cold of winter, clammy and thick.

'I'll be back for you when I have the crystal!'

Jac heard the shout from Ivan and Jac hoped it meant he was gone. Had he taken Gabbi with him? He stood motionless, watching, and waiting while the smoke cleared. He was relieved to see Gabbi lying on the ground and he rushed over to her just as she began to stir.

'What the...' She sat up, groggy, and put her hand to her face. 'That hurts.'

'He's gone,' Jac told her and she looked relieved.

'And the map?' Gabbi pulled herself to her feet and dusted herself off as she looked around for the satchel. Her good humour vanished as she realised it wasn't there and she turned on Jac with a rage that made him jump. 'What did you do? You didn't give it to him did you?'

'He was going to hurt you,' Jac started to explain. He wanted to say he could draw them another one but she didn't give him a chance.

'You fool!' She stamped her foot and glared at

him angrily. 'That map was far more important than me.'

'What?' Jac wasn't sure he was hearing this. She was angry with him for saving her!

'I suppose it could have been worse. He might have taken you too,' Gabbi muttered, almost to herself as she stomped off out of the clearing. Jac got the feeling that she wasn't worried if he was following or not and he stayed a good distance behind her.

Jac was pleased to see three horses racing up to them when they came out of the woods. Danel, Zora and Trel pulled up their mounts just as he and Gabbi reached Kimi.

'You should have let me come,' Kimi rumbled angrily. 'I could have helped.'

'He's too dangerous,' Gabbi replied bluntly and turned to the three new arrivals.

'Did you get it?' Trel asked as he jumped down from his horse. When he saw the sober expression on Gabbi's face he scowled.

'He gave it to Ivan,' Gabbi spat the words out with disgust and threw herself up onto Kimi's back as she shot a nasty look at Jac.

'You knew how important it was,' Zora said in an exasperated tone.

'I was trying to save Gabbi,' Jac defended himself. 'I can draw you another one.'

Jac got a stick and traced several of the lines in

the ground. It was dusty out here so the rain had obviously not reached this far out.

'See!' Jac pointed at the ground feeling pleased that he had remembered it so accurately.

'That's no use to us at all,' Gabbi said without even the barest glance at his drawing.

'A copy won't do,' Zora explained, a little less angry, realising he had intended well. 'Only the original map can help us find it.'

'But it looks just like the one in the satchel,' Jac protested, not understanding why a copy would be useless.

'The crystal moves and the map changes as it moves,' Zora told him and patted him on the back as one would a small child. 'The real map is woven by magic.'

'I'll see you back in town, Grandfather.' Gabbi urged Kimi up into the air and without a backwards look she flew off. Jac hadn't expected huge thanks for saving her but he had thought she would be pleased.

'There's no point hanging around here,' Trel said as he mounted again and rode off.

Zora shook her head at him but said nothing as she too turned her horse and rode off. Danel shrugged his shoulders as they both watched everyone leave.

'Want a lift?' he asked and patted the side of his horse gently. 'I don't think they're all that happy with you.'

'I only did what I thought was right,' Jac muttered.

On the ride back into town Jac filled Danel in on the rest of what he knew. The sight that met them back at the circus wasn't what they had expected. They had been gone less than an hour yet so much had changed. The wedding marquee was gone and the big top was being dismantled. Wagons were being loaded up and it looked as if the circus was leaving town.

'What's going on?' Jac said out loud, not really expecting an answer.

'I've no idea but it doesn't look good,' Danel replied. 'I'll take the horse back and you can go and find out what has happened.'

Jac nodded and slipped from the horse's back. He walked over to where the bigtop was fast becoming just a huge bundle of canvas. He moved into position next to Otis and began helping to fold the huge tent.

'What's up?' Jac said casually, as if it was nothing out of the ordinary to be packing up so soon after arriving.

'The wedding's off,' Otis told him as they heaved the canvas. 'And we've been ordered to leave town.'

'Off?' Jac repeated. Why? He didn't have to wonder for long as Mr Blyne stormed over towards him with a look of thunder on his face.

'Jac! Get out of my circus!' He bellowed before he had even reached Jac. 'Get out now!'

'Don't take it out on the boy.' Otis stood up and put himself between the ringmaster and Jac.

'The king hated the puppets and so did Prince Bradley!' Mr Blyne roared and roughly pushed Otis out of the way. The ringmaster pulled at Jac's shirt, forcing him to lean down. 'If I see you near my circus ever again…'

He left the threat hanging and walked off in the direction of Jac's wagon.

'He'll calm down,' Otis said comfortingly as Jac stared after him.

'I don't think so,' Jac replied. 'I think it's time I left the circus anyway.'

Jac shook Otis' extended hand and with a weak grin of farewell he walked off after the ringmaster. Well that explained why they were leaving town but not why the wedding had been called off. Not liking a present wasn't a reason to cancel a wedding, so something else must have happened - but what?

Jac pushed it to the back of his mind as he got closer to the wagon. He had other problems to think about just now, lots of them. He cringed as he approached the wagon and saw the hole was even bigger. It was swallowing the entire river now and was only a few feet from the wagons.

Several people were staring at it from a safe distance and Jac detoured around them. One of his other problems was watching out of the wagon window, well two of them actually, Dan and Lotte.

The ringmaster was striding off as Jac arrived and the little dwarf didn't even look up. Zora stood on the steps, frowning, but it wasn't directed at Jac.

'I don't like leaving without fixing that,' she said as she pointed at the hole. 'Someone could get hurt.'

Well that was an understatement if ever he heard one. A bottomless hole was spreading across the lowlands, swallowing anything that got in its way and she was worried someone might get hurt!

Gabbi's wagon, pulling Kimi's cage behind it, rumbled up and stopped next to them. Trel was sitting on the driving seat with her and he looked grim.

'Are you ready?' Gabbi asked Zora bluntly.

'We don't need to go where you go,' Zora stated defensively.

'Where are you going?' Trel asked and raised one eyebrow in question.

'We need to see the tomes held at Mage City to find a way to stop that,' Zora pointed at the hole.

'That's where we're going,' Gabbi stated. 'To

see if there's any other way to find the crystal without the map.'

'Then I guess we'll see you there,' Zora replied a little bluntly. Jac knew he had two reasons for going to Mage City. One was to help find a way to fix the hole… and to make sure he was the first one to find the Star Crystal.

The horse was hitched and in just a few minutes they were heading out of the field and onto the cobbled road. Jac looked back, trying to see if he could see Danel. He hadn't even had a chance to say goodbye to his friend or even tell him he was leaving.

CHAPTER ELEVEN
ROOM FOR ONE MORE

Jac lost sight of Sweetwater over an hour before noon and he slouched in the driving seat, holding the reins lightly and letting the horse trot along gently. Gabbi and her grandfather were a little way ahead of them now and Zora kept checking they were in sight. She had just gone into the wagon, claiming she was tired, but not before telling Jac to make sure he kept close behind Gabbi.

He had no idea where Mage City was but as long as he followed Gabbi's wagon he must be going the right way. Dan and Lotte were sitting up front with him and Jac scowled with disgust at their excited and happy faces. What was there to be happy about? At least that horrible puppet, Brad, was still asleep.

'Faster.' Dan poked Jac in the stomach and Jac wriggled out of his reach.

'I don't want to catch up to them.' Jac pointed up ahead and Dan poked him again.

'Lotte wants to see the dragon,' he insisted.

'Don't worry, I'm sure we'll be seeing lots of it,' Jac assured him. Lotte seemed to be a nice natured puppet, much like Dan, and Dan had taken on the role of protector and companion to her. She looked shyly at Jac whenever he turned her way but she hadn't spoken to him.

They continued travelling for most of the day, going steadily upwards as they neared the huge mountains that marked the end of the lowlands. It was early evening when Dan sat up and gasped in horror.

'Dragon gone!' he said, jumping to stand on the seat and staring ahead of them.

Jac took a quick look around before relaxing back into the seat.

'It's just the mountain pass,' he explained. 'You can't see them when they go around the corner. Once we're round it you'll see them again.'

The horse slowed down automatically as they neared the hairpin bend in the road. To one side the mountain dropped away to a sheer cliff and the road narrowed to a width that didn't look wide enough to drive a wagon on. It seemed to end in another drop straight ahead of them and anyone not knowing there was a bend in the road would not venture any further.

The horse was well trained and it didn't even falter in its step as it moved confidently towards the corner. Dan and Lotte almost leapt onto Jac's knee when they saw the steep drop and Jac patted them reassuringly.

'It's wide enough, don't worry the horse has done this dozens of times.' Jac could well remember when he was small and the corner seemed impossible to get around. 'Just shut your eyes and I'll tell you when we're through the pass.'

Both puppets squeezed their eyes shut as Jac guided the horse slowly around the sharp bend and he waited until the rock was high on both sides before he told them to open their eyes. He could see the relief in their eyes and Dan looked delighted to see Kimi's wagon not far up ahead.

The pass opened out to a flat plateau and the view over the highlands was breath-taking. Gabbi and her grandfather had stopped up near a stream that ran swiftly down the mountain. It was where the circus always stopped on their trip through the mountains and even though Jac didn't really want to camp next to them there was nowhere else to stop. They needed fresh water for the horse and the shelter that the high walls of the pass entrance offered. Often the winds up this high were swift and harsh. Once they had to wait three days for weather calm enough to make the passage around the hairpin bend.

Jac stopped the wagon a short distance from Gabbi's, there was no need to stop right next to them, and he helped the puppets down from the front seat.

'Can I take Lotte over to see the dragon?' Dan asked, clinging tightly to Lotte's little hand.

'I don't see why not,' Jac shrugged. Kimi was probably lonely if all she had for company was a grumpy Gabbi and the old man. 'Just don't upset the lady.'

Dan nodded seriously and led Lotte off across the bare ground, leading her around the bigger rocks as if she needed his guidance.

Jac turned to the task of unhitching the horse and he led it down near the river. He waited while it drank its fill and then tethered it to one of the few trees that struggled to survive there.

As Jac walked back to the wagon a loud shouting and rumbling came from behind him. Zora came out of the wagon and they both turned to see what was going on and Jac realised that it was coming from the mountain pass. Someone was coming around from the dwarf side... and they were coming fast. If they didn't slow down they wouldn't make it round.

Was it someone from the circus? Jac knew that Ivan would have to use this pass as well if he was travelling north but he doubted that Ivan would be making so much noise or travelling so fast. Gabbi and Trel came out of their wagon to watch as well and the puppets hurried back to shelter under the safety of Jac's wagon.

A horse's head appeared around the corner, and Jac knew instantly that it was going too fast. There was no way the wagon would turn fast enough at that speed. There was a sliding sound as the wagon behind it tried to follow the horse's swift turn. Jac was sure he wasn't the only one to hold his breath as the wagon came into sight, with Mr Blyne at the reins.

The wagon seemed to slide most of the way around the bend as the ringmaster kept thrashing at the horse with the reins, seemingly mindless of the danger he was in. It seemed as if the wagon would make it around but the back wheels slid over the edge of the path and hovered in mid air before hitting the side of the pass and bouncing wildly up into the air. The wagon tilted forward as the poor horse tried to wrench itself free of the out of control wagon.

The wagon banged back down on the rear wheels, smashing them instantly but Mr Blyne didn't even pause to see that his wagon was dragging along on only two wheels. His face was a picture of anguish and fear as he urged his horse on, completely ignoring those who stood watching.

The rest of the circus wagons came around the mountain pass, much more slowly and without further damage, as Mr Blyne slid to a halt not far from Jac and the others. Danel was the last to come around the pass, on the wood wagon as usual, and he drew up right next to Jac.

'The king accused us of kidnapping the

princess. Then he saw that hole and said we had done it to destroy him,' Danel told him and then shook his head. 'It's getting huge Jac.'

Jac didn't comment. At least that explained why the wedding had been called off. A wedding with no bride was rather difficult.

'Anyway, he decided that we should all be thrown into the dungeons, or that hole, and we all took off.' Danel pointed back towards the mountain pass. 'They were still following us an hour ago but hopefully we lost them before we got to the pass.'

'So you're all going to the highlands in the winter?' Jac asked. Nobody went to a circus in the winter so Mr Blyne would be in for a very poor season.

'I don't know, maybe we'll just wait here a while and when they find their princess we'll go back,' Danel replied lightly as he jumped down from the wagon. 'Anyway why did you take off?'

'The king didn't like the puppets so we got kicked out,' Jac explained. He glanced over at the other wagon and saw that Gabbi had gone back inside but Trel sat on the steps of the wagon, staring in his direction. Jac turned his back on the old man, feeling very unsettled at being watched by someone who feared his very existence.

'I'd better go and help set up camp,' Danel said as he flicked the reins lightly. 'I'll come back later.'

Just as Danel drove off a voice came from within Jac's wagon that made Jac sigh.

'Let me out!'

That rotten grumpy puppet had woken up. Zora opened the wagon door and Dan and Lotte shot up the steps from their hiding place under the wagon. Jac went in just as Zora was freeing Brad from the sack while Dan and Lotte stood back a good distance.

This time Brad didn't come out yelling and angry. He looked sullenly around at them all and then backed away under a chair.

'You'll have to let me go sooner or later,' he muttered so softly that Jac only just heard it. He wasn't too brave when he realised he was outnumbered.

Jac left Zora to watch them while he started a fire as it was colder up here in the mountains. Further down in the highlands it was winter too and since they couldn't go back to the lowlands for a while they would have to get used to the cold. He wondered how far away Mage City was but didn't see any point in asking right now. He just had to hope they got there before Ivan got hold of the Star Crystal. Maybe giving him the map hadn't been such a good idea after all, but what choice did he have at the time?

His mother came out and set some water to boil

over the fire. 'Brad is still under the chair, claiming that we've kidnapped him but since he can't reach the door handle I don't think he'll go anywhere.

It was getting on for dusk when a figure came towards them from the direction of the circus. His eyes were temporarily blinded from looking into the flames and he took a cautious step backwards, was it Ivan? He relaxed with a nervous laugh when he realised that it was just Danel.

'Got room for one more?' Danel asked soberly as he hovered at the edge of the firelight.

'Did Blyne kick you out too?' Jac asked in surprise.

'Nope, but I've had enough of the circus. Your life looks far more interesting anyway,' Danel said with a hint of his usual cheeky grin.

'You can have it, willingly,' Jac offered and then looked to see if his mother had been listening to Danel.

'There's always room for one more,' she replied without even looking up. 'I can't guarantee you'll like where we're going but you're welcome to come if you want.'

'It's got to be better than the circus,' Danel said with a sigh of relief. 'Jac, wanna come and help me pack?'

Jac fell into step with his friend as they

approached the cluster of wagons from the back. They walked in companionable silence and just as they were almost at the wagons Danel stopped and grabbed at Jac's shirt.

'Look, isn't that Albot?' Danel nudged Jac and pointed over to Mr Blyne's wagon. Albot was coming down the steps, dressed in travelling clothes and wearing a large pack on his back.

'I wonder where dear old Albot is going.' Jac muttered and after checking that nobody was around he hurried over to intercept him. If he was leaving the circus then this might be his last chance to get Kimi's gems back. He felt guilty that he hadn't even told Gabbi who it was that stole them. Jac grabbed Albot's arm and he looked up at Jac in surprise.

'Where are you going, Albot?' Danel asked, following him over and grabbing Albot's other arm, pinning him to the back of the wagon.

'I just… Well… I'm going to… Let me go! I don't have to answer any of your questions.' Albot squirmed free and his left hand went immediately to his trouser pocket.

'You got something valuable there?' Jac asked, perhaps it was Kimi's gems.

'Nothing to concern you,' Albot said angrily.

'I think you've got something that you stole from a friend of mine,' Jac said and Albot went pale and began to shake.

'A friend of yours! Here, take it! Just leave me be!' Albot's face went a horrible shade of white that seemed to glow in the half-light of dusk. He pulled a small bag on a thin cord out of his pocket, threw it on the ground and ran off between the wagons.

CHAPTER TWELVE
A FAST HORSE

'It doesn't look like gems,' Jac said as he picked up the small bag. It was made of a supple hide that had been roughly stitched together at the sides but it didn't feel as if there were gems in it.

'Someone's coming,' Danel warned and they moved away from the wagon and around to Danel's.

It wasn't until they had collected Danel things and were back at the fire that Jac had a chance to look properly at the bag.

'There's nothing in it!' Jac muttered as he shook the bag upside down in disgust. 'The gems probably fell out in his pocket.'

Jac threw the bag onto the dry grass-tufted ground and sank down cross-legged next to the fire. Dan and Lotte were sitting opposite and Dan eyed the bag with interest.

'Can I have it?' he asked without moving towards it.

'Sure,' Jac replied with a shrug of his shoulders and then turned to Danel to check that he didn't mind.

'It's of no use to us,' Danel agreed. 'Be careful what you put in it though as it doesn't look very well made.'

Dan broke into a grin that showed off a row of perfect wooden teeth and he scuttled quickly around the fire to retrieve the bag. He hurried back to Lotte's side and they both ran their hands over the bag in wonder.

'I guess that's the first thing he's owned,' Jac mused as he watched the delighted look on the little puppet's face. Dan slipped the thin cord over his shoulder and the bag missed dragging on the ground by a matter of a few inches.

Gabbi and Trel kept their distance that night and Jac was glad. He didn't really know what to say to Gabbi anyway. She considered him someone to be afraid of, someone who needed to be removed from everyone's life as quickly as possible. Sleep didn't come easily that night for Jac and he spent a long time staring out the wagon window at the stars. He finally nodded off and it seemed like only minutes later that he heard a voice calling to him.

Jac.

He sat up and looked around in the dimly lit wagon. Nobody else was awake not even the bad tempered Brad, who had curled up under the chair by the door, probably intending to make a dash for freedom as soon as the door opened. A small lamp on the table reflected dully on his face and even in sleep he looked bad-tempered and sour.

Jac.

There it was again. He looked at each face, his mind still groggy with sleep, until he realised that the voice came from within his mind.

Kimi? Jac queried back, finding it odd to speak without moving his lips.

They have gone already. Kimi's voice came back, growing fainter with each word.

'Who has gone?' Jac asked out loud and the two puppets at the end of his bed stirred in their sleep. He propped himself up to look out the window but clouds covered the moon and he couldn't see very far at all.

They will cause you trouble… Kimi's voice faded away completely. Kimi was gone and that meant Gabbi and Trel had gone as well. The old man wanted to keep a close eye on him so why would he suddenly up and leave in the middle of the night?

Jac considered waking his mother but finally decided that until they knew which way they had gone there was little point in worrying her. They wouldn't know until morning when they would be able to see where their tracks went so he lay back down and was asleep within seconds.

'Jac!'

He was roughly shaken from his dream and he opened his eyes, startled and cautious. Danel was standing by his bed, dressed and with a cup of hot soup in his hand.

'I thought you'd never wake up,' Danel said as he shoved the soup into Jac's hand. 'It's well after dawn and Gabbi has gone already.'

'Which way did they go?' Jac asked as he rubbed his eyes with his free hand and blew on his soup.

'It's a bit hard to tell since the circus just pulled out as well and all the tracks are a mess.' Dan shrugged his shoulders in an apology for not being able to tell. 'But your mother looks worried even though she said she knows where they are heading.'

'They're going to Mage City,' Jac told him. He pulled himself to a sitting position and squinted out into the bright light of day through the window. 'You should have woken me earlier.'

'We tried,' Danel replied sourly. 'Dan even jumped up and down on the bed but you just snored on.'

'I don't snore,' Jac objected and he swung his legs over the bed to stand up. 'Where are the puppets?'

'Dan and Lotte are up front with your mother, and the other one is still under that chair,' Danel said with a sigh as he pointed over to the chair. Brad had knocked over a small stool and barricaded himself into the corner. All Jac could see were his eyes glaring out at them with an unreadable expression.

Jac felt the unmistakable shake of the wagon that meant the horse was being hitched up. He drank the soup in one go and handed the cup back to Danel. He hurried out of the wagon to help get ready to leave. A quick glance around once he was outside told him that theirs was the only wagon left in the small clearing. Even the remains of the fire had gone and when they left there would be no sign that anyone had been here except for some faint wheel tracks that would be gone within a day; covered by the winds that roared up the pass.

'I wonder how long ago they left,' his mother mused out loud as she allowed Jac to take over seeing to the horse.

'It was still full dark,' Jac said and when his mother raised an eyebrow in question he continued. 'Kimi woke me up to tell me.'

'You should have woken me,' his mother said with a shake of her head. 'They've got a good head start on us.'

'But we know where they are going.' Jac felt confused and a little ashamed that he hadn't woken her when he thought about it earlier.

'Oh yes, I know exactly where they are going. But if they get there before us there will be trouble, big trouble.' Zora patted the horse affectionately as she gathered up the reins and climbed up onto the driving seat, pushing the two puppets along to make room.

Jac finished checking the straps as Danel came out of the wagon and climbed up onto the driving seat, pulling the two puppets onto his knees.

'Sorry,' Jac muttered to his mother as he climbed up to take the last space on the seat.

'There would have been trouble anyway, it just would have been better if we arrived with them or even before them.' Zora smiled at him and Jac knew she wasn't angry. She flicked the reins and the horse walked forward obediently. 'We'll just deal with it when we get there.'

Instead of circling around and heading down the pass towards the highlands she drove the horse straight towards the fast flowing river. The horse stopped just short of the cold, swiftly flowing river but Zora urged it forward and it reluctantly stepped into the chilly water.

Jac wondered why they were crossing the river for there was nothing on the other side except for sheer rock walls, jagged and uneven with many deep crevices. They emerged from the river on the small strip of ground that formed the other bank and the horse stamped its feet. Zora flicked the reins again and they moved forward again towards one of the crevices. It was then that Jac noticed the faint marks of wheels and hooves coming out of the stream just next to them; so Gabbi had gone this way too.

Jac held his questions and they were answered almost immediately as they drove straight into the biggest crevice and he was shocked to realise that it too concealed a pass through the mountain. He knew he shouldn't really have been surprised though, for if there was one pass then why shouldn't there be others?

They cleared the high walls of the narrow pass within a few minutes and it opened out to a gradual slope that led down into a lush green forest. There was a definite path leading directly up from the forest. People on this side of the mountain pass must all know about its existence for it could not be mistaken for a natural landmark and it looked well used.

'How far ahead do you think they are?' Jac asked. There was no way they would see them up ahead in the miles of forest they would have to go through. The city they were heading for wasn't in sight either.

'It's about a three hour ride from here so they might be almost there if they left in full dark,' Zora replied absently as she stared off across the tops of the trees. 'I imagine they'll send someone to find us before we get that far.'

'Can't we catch up?' Danel asked. He still had the two puppets on his knee and they wriggled to stand up for a better view.

'I wish we could,' Jac muttered almost to himself. He was about to add that they would have to just about fly when he felt the wagon lurch forward. He looked over at his mother but she looked just as surprised at the sudden movement.

'It must have been a rock,' Zora commented, scanning the track ahead for any more. They all knew that striking a rock could mean a broken wheel and cause even more delays.

Jac felt the wagon lurch again and they all looked at each other and the then at the horse. It seemed to be walking along at the normal pace but something else didn't seem right. They were going down the slope much too fast.

Zora pulled on the reins to slow the horse down but their speed just increased even though the horse seemed to respond to the command. The horse threw its head and whinnied in confusion as the ground disappeared far too quickly under its hooves.

'What's happening?' Danel asked nobody in particular as he struggled to keep hold of the puppets with the wagon picking up speed by the second.

'I don't know,' Zora replied. She had stopped trying to control the horse and the reins lay limply across her lap.

'I guess we might catch up with Gabbi after all,' Danel commented as he watched the trees get closer and closer at an alarming rate. 'If we make it through the forest without crashing.'

'Jac wished it,' Dan said calmly as he held his arms up to catch the wind that rushed at them.

Jac frowned briefly and then realised that Dan was right. He had wished they would get to the city before Gabbi and now it was happening. He was beginning to understand a little about how his magic worked. If he wanted something badly enough it seemed to happen. He had wanted Dan to be real and then he had wanted Dan to have friends, even it was only briefly. Surely it wouldn't be too hard to control magic that worked like that?

'I guess I did,' Jac admitted a little apologetically and turned to face his mother. 'Do you want me to try to slow us down?'

'No,' Zora replied slowly with a thoughtful look on her face. 'I don't see that this can do any harm.'

They all held their breath as the forest rushed up to them and then they were racing headlong through the trees. Old wizened barks whistled past only inches from the sides of the wagon and hanging vines whipped against their faces.

'Perhaps I should slow us down a little,' Jac said as he fought off a low hanging branch.

'We're almost out of the forest,' Zora pointed out and only seconds later they all burst out onto the grasslands. A sea of long thin grass waved gently for as far as he could see. The road was wider now and cut a path straight through the grass. Their pace hadn't slowed down at all and if anything they were going faster now that they were clear of the deadly vines and branches.

They all sat without talking, watching in wonder as they hurtled along the straight road. The horse had accepted the speed and was keeping a steady pace even though its hooves were barely touching the ground.

'How far?' Danel asked as the ground rose up sharply before them.

'Just over the rise,' Zora replied, looking immensely pleased with their speedy trip. 'Jac, now might be a good time to slow us down. If the mages see us arriving at this speed it will do just as much damage as Gabbi and Trel could have done by arriving first.'

'But they might be there already,' Jac pointed out. He was proven wrong as they reached the top of the small hill and Gabbi's wagon could clearly be seen ahead of them. She was still a good distance from a huge walled city that lay almost on the horizon and even without magical speed they would easily be able to catch up to them. Jac concentrated on slowing them down and sighed with relief, along with everyone else, when the wagon resumed a natural gentle pace. The only one who didn't seem happy was the horse, after a few shuddering pulls at the reins it shouldered the weight of the wagon once again and they set off after Gabbi.

Gabbi has seen you. She is cross.

Kimi's voice came clearly into Jac's mind and he almost chuckled at the thought of ruining her plans to make trouble for him. The great walled city loomed up ahead of them as they finally caught up with Gabbi, Trel and Kimi. The sheer size of the walls seemed unbelievable and it wasn't until they were alongside Gabbi that he realised there were people walking along the top of them, laying even more rows of blocks on top of it.

'You made good time,' Gabbi almost grunted at them.

'It's a fast horse,' Jac replied calmly.

'Were you planning a welcoming committee for us?' Zora queried politely but received no answer.

They continued in silence until they were within a few wagon lengths of the wall. They drew to a stop just short of a wide river that ran round the walls of the city. To Jac there seemed to be no way to cross it and he wondered if they had come upon the city from the wrong side. A small door halfway up the wall opened and a man stepped out onto a small ledge. He wore flowing robes, a lot like Ivan's but white in colour, and he carried a wooden staff which was taller than him by half again. His face was so wrinkled that it was difficult to see if he was smiling or frowning. A long flowing beard of pure white hung limply down to the ground, slightly blackened at the tip.

'Halt! Who wishes to enter the city of mages?'

He slammed the staff down against the stone portal, causing a crack of thunder to roll past them and off across the sky.

'We do, Gatekeeper,' Trel announced loudly. 'We come to seek answers to our questions.'

The old man stepped back and a drawbridge began to lower. All of a sudden it stopped and went back up.

'Wait.' The gatekeeper held up his staff and then pointed it directly at Jac. 'I feel something.'

His eyes bored into Jac across the river and Jac wriggled uncomfortably in his seat.

'Yes, my son is gifted.' Zora spoke loudly and stood up on the footboard to draw the gatekeeper's attention.

The gatekeeper drew in a sharp breath and even with all the creases on his face he managed to look shocked. Jac was sure he saw him take a small step backwards and a flash of fear cross his face.

'You bring him here before he has been cleansed? Take him away until he is safe to be amongst us.' The gatekeeper bristled with indignation and slammed his staff into the stone again. Thunder rolled around them for a second time but Zora did not move.

'He is no danger to you,' she stated firmly.

'We come to track down the Star Crystal. Without it we cannot cleanse him.' Trel spoke again and the gatekeeper barely flicked his attention over to the old archmage.

'Shield his magic. Then I will allow him to pass into the city,' the gatekeeper demanded bluntly of Zora.

'He will not harm you or anyone else in the city,' Zora objected quickly.

'Shield him… or I will.' The gatekeeper glared at Zora. Zora stared back and for a long minute neither would give any ground. Finally, Zora pursed her lips and nodded briefly. A movement so small that Jac wondered how the gatekeeper had seen it from where he was.

'I'm sorry Jac,' Zora said as she turned to face her son. 'There's no other way.'

Jac frowned, wondering what she meant, but a second later he knew and his eyes widened with shock and he almost leaped to his feet.

CHAPTER THIRTEEN
CITY OF MAGES

Jac had felt like this before and never known why. It seemed as if he were watching everything from a distance. Sounds seemed sharper, yet further away, and the world around him seemed less real than it had a few seconds ago. Many times he had felt this as a child and wondered what was wrong with him. It didn't exactly hurt but it made him feel as if he wasn't really in full control. He pushed his conscious mind against the invisible barrier that was blocking him from the real world but it held firmly.

'Don't fight it, Jac,' Zora cautioned him quietly. 'If they realise your magic is stronger than mine they will do far more to you than this small shield. As long as you don't try to use your magic you won't even notice anything.'

Jac nodded once and then relaxed back into his seat, mutely accepting his fate for now. He knew his mother would not have done it if she had any other choice. Slowly his vision returned to normal and the world came back into focus.

The gatekeeper stepped back through his small wooden door, closing it firmly, and the drawbridge began to lower once more.

'Will everyone be that afraid of me?' Jac asked

softly as the drawbridge banged into place. Zora waited while Gabbi and Trel crossed first and then slapped the reins lightly against the horse.

'Yes, some even more so. If Gabbi and Trel had arrived first they would have built upon that fear so that they would have not even given me the chance to shield you myself.' Zora set her mouth in a firm line that hid her own worries. 'We take a chance, bringing you here, but we need to find a way to stop that hole and here is the only place that we might find the answer.'

'I'm not afraid of you Jac,' Danel said and he punched Jac hard on the arm, grinning as he ducked out of the way of Jac's response.

The wagon rolled slowly across the wooden bridge and into the Mage City. It wasn't at all what Jac had expected though. From the outside nothing could be seen and he had thought it to be just a city of buildings and streets but instead they drove out into lush green countryside with farms and cottages dotted over the gently rolling hills. The road ran alongside a swift flowing, but shallow river and men were using floating barges to move huge slabs of stone down towards the wall.

'Why does it need to be so high?' Danel asked as they watched the stones float by.

'The council of elders fear the city will be attacked one day,' Zora replied with a shrug.

'By who?' Jac couldn't help but express his surprise. Who would take on a city full of magical wizards? He looked back at the wall to see if the gatekeeper was watching them but there was no sign of him.

'I've no idea.' Zora didn't seem to be listening any longer as she looked out over a hill that brought them into view of the main city ahead. A mass of buildings lay huddled at the foot of a huge mountain, some of the buildings were built into the side of the mountain as far as half way up. The only reason they hadn't seen the mountain from back at the wall was that it lay deep in a valley and the top of the mountain was only just higher than where they now stood.

Gabbi and Trel were almost half way down the winding valley road and from the dust that was flying from their wheels they were obviously in a hurry to be the first ones into the main area of the city.

It took almost half an hour to reach the outskirts of the large city, which from a distance had looked tiny, and the dirt road changed to a well worn cobbled one.

Jac stared at the sight that greeted them. He had never seen so many buildings or so many people either. Children ran along the narrow streets, some chasing a ball, others sat staring at the newcomers, wide-eyed and unblinking. Adults hurried about in all different directions, some dragging unwilling children after them, others with baskets of food or sacks with indefinable lumps in them.

Only a few people took any notice of them as Zora drove the wagon slowly through the crowded streets. Jac frowned as a man hefting a large barrel stopped to allow them to pass. He barely even acknowledged their passing, just paused long enough for them to pass and then continued walking, his expression unchanged and blank.

'Some of the people here...' Jac began but his mother shook her head quickly.

'Not right now Jac. I'll explain later,' she said with a warning glance.

Jac fell silent but couldn't shake the feeling that something was terribly wrong. Zora pulled the wagon to a stop outside a building which was smaller than most of the others. A battered wooden sign hung above the door and it gave Jac little comfort.

'The Flying Jug!' Danel commented as they climbed down from the seat. 'Doesn't sound promising.'

'I wouldn't stay anywhere else,' Zora remarked quietly as she handed the reins of the horse to a young girl who came quietly around the side of the building. Zora paused much longer than was necessary, as if waiting for the girl to acknowledge her.

Jac couldn't help notice that the girl didn't look like a normal stable hand. She had long, straight black hair that swept down to her waist and pale, delicate skin that was covered in smears of dirt and several bruises. Her heavy woollen dress hung loosely and untidily as if she didn't care how she looked. Zora heaved a silent sigh as she went into the inn, followed by Danel and the two puppets. Jac hesitated as he felt drawn to watch the girl for some unknown reason.

She didn't seem afraid of the horse but she didn't seem to know how to handle it either. She tugged at the reins in an attempt to get it to follow her around the side but it remained where it was. She kept her face cast down towards the ground as she continued to tug ineffectively.

'Let me show you how to get her to move.' Jac walked over and took the reins from her and then stopped in shock as she turned her face up to look at him. It wasn't that she was unattractive, for she was a pretty girl of about his own age; it was her eyes that made him suck in his breath. Her eyes were the blue of a summer sky with small flecks of black. It was the emptiness behind them made a shiver run down his back. She looked straight at him but didn't seem to hear his words.

'Just flick the reins like this…' Jac said woodenly as he flicked them and handed them back to her. The horse began to move forward and the girl turned away without even blinking, leading the horse, tugging as she had been before.

'Come inside, Jac.'

Jac turned to see his mother standing in the doorway of the Inn with a look of sadness and sympathy clear on her face. He followed her into the dimly lit building knowing he would have to wait for an explanation. Clearly it was something that she couldn't tell him in public.

The inside of the Inn was exactly what the sign outside promised. Straw, old and stained, covered the stone floor. Sturdy wooden tables were bolted to the floor around the sides of the room and Jac doubted that the space in the middle was left for dancing. Only a couple of people sat at the tables and they were more interested in the contents of their jugs than the people walking past them.

'Zora, it's been a long time.' A small woman with a chubby, happy face came up to greet them. She was drying her hands on a dirty rag and the smell of fresh baking reached Jac's nose. Danel had obviously smelt it as well for he was practically drooling.

'Tessa, it's good to see you again.' The two women hugged briefly and then Tessa turned to look at Jac and Danel.

'Which one...' she settled her gaze on Jac and then nodded. 'He's grown.'

'It's been ten summers,' Zora pointed out. 'Melanie has grown so much I almost didn't recognise her.'

'We've had to get her tending the horses lately. She was working in here but she spilled too much ale,' Tessa replied with a sigh that stripped the happiness from her face. 'It's not going well though. She takes so long to learn something new.'

A shout for more ale dragged her attention from them for a split second then she turned back. She fished into the deep pocket of her dirty apron and tossed a small object to Zora. 'Second left at the top of the stairs.'

Zora caught the key and they followed her to the small stairs at the back of the Inn. The room Zora led them to was small but clean and she locked the door behind them as soon as they were all inside.

'Jac,' she turned to him and then seemed at a loss for what to say. 'It's like this...'

'What's wrong with Melanie and those other people we saw?' Jac asked when she fell silent again.

'Nothing is actually 'wrong' with them,' Zora replied evasively and then she gave a huge sigh.

'It's what's missing.'

'Missing?' Danel echoed but Jac had already grasped his mother's meaning.

'They were gifted too weren't they?' he demanded almost harshly. 'Is that what I would be like if Gabbi and Trel find the Star Crystal before us?'

Zora simply nodded, unable to look her son in the eye. The room fell silent as nobody knew what to say next. Dan and Lotte wriggled free of Danel and ran off to jump on the bed. It was then that Jac noticed that Brad wasn't with them. He didn't really mind if the bad tempered puppet stayed in the wagon a while longer but it gave him the excuse he needed.

'I'm going down to the wagon to get Brad.' Jac didn't wait to see if anybody was going to object. He wanted to go and see Melanie again. He found her easily enough for the stables were directly behind the Inn. She had managed to get the wagon under the shelter of the barn but hadn't unhitched the horse yet. She was pulling on one of the straps and seemed unaware that she was tightening them. The horse flinched but stood her ground while the straps dug into her.

Jac paused at the entrance to the barn. A feeling of deep pity welling up within him as he hurried forward to help her. Slowly and gently he tried to guide her hands to unhitch the horse and then helped to lead it into a stall. He secured the latch on the gate and then watched as Melanie managed to set a bowl of water within the horse's reach.

'Melanie.' Jac turned the dark-haired girl to face him. He looked eagerly at her eyes, her face, hoping for some recognition of her name. Empty eyes looked back at him yet they looked oddly familiar. He was sure he'd seen her somewhere before. 'I'm Jac.'

For the briefest of seconds Jac was sure he saw something deep inside her eyes, barely even a flicker, but it was there.

'Jac.' He repeated and again he saw the flicker of life. She wasn't just the mindless drudge that Tessa seemed to think. Melanie was still there inside her and Jac knew he was going to find a way to bring her back.

'Jac,' Danel's voice came from the other side of the wagon and he turned to see his friend holding Brad. 'I found him running up the alleyway.'

It was tempting to just let Brad run off, he certainly didn't want to be around them, but Jac knew that wasn't an option. He had brought Brad to life and he was responsible for him.

'Zora says we've got to go to the archive. Gabbi and Trel have probably already gone there.' Danel deftly stopped the wriggling puppet from biting him and held him at arms length. 'What should I do with this one?'

'It's his choice,' Jac said with a sigh. 'Either he behaves himself and comes with us or he goes back in the wagon.'

Brad glared at Jac defiantly but didn't reply.

'Put him in the wagon,' Jac said. He turned to see what Melanie was doing and he was surprised to find that she was standing directly behind him, exactly where she had been before. He didn't expect her to understand but he couldn't just walk off without saying goodbye. 'I have to go.'

Jac walked out of the barn and Danel caught up to him before he was halfway across the flagstone courtyard.

'You've made a friend,' Danel commented and shook his head in the direction of the barn. Jac turned and saw Melanie standing staring after them. Zora was waiting out front. She had the two puppets and she handed them one each.

It was only a short walk across the city to where the buildings were cleaner, taller and well-dressed people walked purposely from one building to another. Jac felt the skin on his back suddenly crawl with a feeling of being watched. He stopped and turned, looking around at the faces, but nobody seemed to be taking any notice of them. He was about to put it down to nerves when a movement caught his eye. A flick of a black cloak disappearing into an alley told him what he didn't want to know. Ivan was in the city as well. He didn't know if he should tell his mother and he still hadn't decided when she spoke to him.

'That's the Archive,' Zora said as she pointed to a small building that seemed trapped between two larger ones. Gabbi's wagon was parked outside it and to Jac's annoyance Kimi was still in her cage with the bars drawn down firmly. 'We've no time for that now Jac.'

Jac pressed his lips together in frustration. His mother always seemed to know what he was thinking. He tried to send a silent message to Kimi that he would come back but an overwhelming sense of dizziness overcame him and he had to steady himself on Danel, almost dropping Dan onto the stones.

'I told you not to do that.' Zora turned and helped him up the remaining steps and his head began to clear.

He only vaguely saw the huge wooden doors that led into the Archive but when he saw what was inside he drew in a sharp breath. The ceiling was many times higher than that of the entrance and an unseen light source filled the room with a slightly dimmer light that took a few seconds to adjust to. The room was so large that Jac could only just make out the far side. He wasn't sure how the ceiling could be so high in a building that was clearly not that tall.

Long rows of shelves covered the floor and from where they stood, at the top of the steps that led down into it, it looked to be a maze. From the centre of the maze a thin metal-looking staircase rose twisting up to the ceiling. Jac had only ever seen two tomes as Zora had two that he had learnt to read from and the sight of so many in one place seemed hard to believe.

'I hope you know where we're supposed to start looking,' Jac muttered, feeling overwhelmed and sure that they could look for three summers and never find what they wanted.

Zora nodded and hurried down the steps to the archive floor. Jac followed, looking at the blur of tomes that were crammed into shelves on the wall as they descended. Gabbi and Trel were nowhere in sight but there were hundreds of places in this archive that they could be. Zora moved quickly across the floor and ran her finger along the spines of the tomes as she walked past the first row of shelves. She turned several times, until they were deep in the maze, and then stopped abruptly.

'We need anything that refers to the Star Crystal,' Zora said as he waved her arm in a wide sweep across a whole section of a large shelf.

'And ones for reversing magic.'

The shelves were much taller and longer than they looked from the top of the stairs and Jac sighed at the huge job ahead of them. His reading was quite good but with only two tomes to practice on it was also limited. Zora had already pulled one from the shelf and was deeply engrossed as she flicked quickly through the pages.

Jac had barely glanced at the first volume on the shelf when a shuffling noise caught his attention.

'Did you hear that?' Jac asked but Danel just shrugged. Both Dan and Lotte had run off down the rows of shelves and Jac wondered if it was one of them.

The shuffle came again and Jac decided not to wait for whoever or whatever it was to come to him. He strode quickly down the row hoping to catch the person; he hoped it was a person, off-guard. Just as he was about to turn the corner he remembered seeing Ivan a few minutes earlier, what if it was him? But it was too late to turn back now and Jac hurtled around the corner.

'What the…?'

Jac almost tripped over a small, bald man sitting cross-legged on the floor wearing a long green robe. A pair of battered glasses perched precariously on the end of the man's nose and he dropped the tome he held as he stared up at Jac.

'Who are you?' the man asked curiously. He stretched and got up slowly, as if he had been sitting down for a very long time.

'I'm Jac,' he replied, not sure if that were enough information to give. 'Who are you?'

The man, who was much older than Jac had first thought, pushed his glasses further up his wrinkled nose and peered at him. His sparse eyebrows lowered and he pressed his lips into such a frown that the ends of his mouth curled almost down to his chin.

'I'm the custodian. You should have told me you were here. You mustn't just wander around.' He looked a little confused and then added. 'I don't remember you, Jac. You are a mage aren't you?'

'Well, sort of,' Jac admitted and before he could add any more the custodian grabbed his arm and stared deep into Jac's eyes. A look of shock changed to pure happiness and glee, bordering on hysteria, which lit up the custodian's face. He reminded Jac of a small child receiving an unexpected present.

'I knew you'd come one day!' he almost bellowed, not letting go of Jac's arm and increasing the pressure as if afraid that he might disappear if he let go.

Zora came hurrying around the corner at the custodian's yelling and almost ran into them.

'You brought me a gifted one! One that hasn't been 'cleansed'.' He almost spat out the last word then he beamed at Zora.

'It's not really what you think,' Zora cautioned the old man. 'My son has a shielding to stop his magic.'

'That won't make any difference.' He waved a hand at Zora, as if dismissing it as unimportant.

'Come. Come.' The custodian pushed roughly past Zora and dragged Jac after him, the strength of his grip belying his apparent age. 'I've waited my whole life to see what's inside it.'

CHAPTER FOURTEEN
THE BOX

Inside it? Inside what? Jac cast an asking glance at Zora as he was pulled away from his mother but she just shrugged as if he should humour the old man. He followed as quickly as he could, more to stop the pain that the custodian's grip was causing than an eagerness to see what it was the old man wanted to show him. They moved deeper and deeper into the maze until Jac was sure they must be about to come out the other side.

'It's up here. Mind that first step.' The custodian spoke so quickly that it took Jac a second to work out what he said. He tripped and only just prevented himself from falling face first into the steps he had seen in the middle of the maze.

Thankfully the steps were only wide enough for one person so the custodian let go of Jac's arm and pushed him up the steps in front of him. Jac rubbed his arm as he climbed the steps. At first he went quite quickly, pushed along by the old man's hand on his back. But as the steps wound around and around in the tight spiral that led upwards, he slowed, feeling dizzy.

'Not far now,' the custodian encouraged him, but did not press him faster than he was going.

'It'll be worth the climb. I'm sure of it.'

Jac trudged slowly up to the top trying not to look down as he knew it would surely freeze him in fear. As long as he kept looking up he'd be okay.

When the steps finally ended Jac gripped the handrail that surrounded the small platform at the top and looked around in confusion. What was there up here to look at? The only thing up here was a small wooden table with a wooden box sitting on it. The ceiling was so low that Jac had to stoop.

'Open it!' the custodian grabbed his arm again and dragged Jac over to the small table. The old man was literally jumping up and down in his excitement and Jac wondered if the platform would hold up to it.

'The box?' Jac asked as he looked at the simple wooden box. Why would he drag him all the way up here to look in a small box?

'We've tried to open it for years but we stopped when we finally deciphered the inscription.' The custodian pointed to the carved symbols that Jac hadn't noticed around the sides of the box. 'It says that only a gifted one may open it.'

Jac stepped forward and placed his hand on the box. There didn't appear to be a lock of any sort on it and he pulled gently on the lid. It opened easily and he grabbed hold of the table as the custodian almost pushed him out of the way in his eagerness to see inside it.

'What is it?' he blurted out, peering into the box but not attempting to put his hands anywhere near it.

Jac put his hand into the box and pulled out the only object in there, a folded piece of softened parchment. He unfolded it and turned it over, confused by the fact that it was completely blank. He tried to hand it over to the custodian but he backed off quickly.

'No, I don't want to touch it. If it's gifted magic then it may destroy me for just touching it,' he said with a furious shake of his head.

'This?' Jac looked at the parchment again. Surely it wasn't dangerous. 'What is it for?'

'You don't know?' The custodian's face fell into a tragic look of dismay.

'No, sorry,' Jac replied a little apologetically, feeling sorry for the old man who had spent so long trying to open the box.

'Close the box when you've finished looking,' the old man grumbled sourly. 'I'm going back to my work.'

With that the custodian stamped off down the steps, rattling the platform alarmingly and forcing Jac to hold on to the table for support. Jac stared at the box which was lined with smooth red velvet.

'It should be deeper,' Jac muttered to himself as he looked at the box from the side and then from the top again. He reached into the small space and with a satisfying click he found the opening to another chamber inside it.

He turned to call to the custodian to tell him to come back up but he had already reached the bottom of the winding steps and disappeared into the maze. Just looking down from this height made Jac feel ill and he withdrew back towards the table again. He would just have to look what it was and then take it down to the custodian if it looked interesting. Whatever it was, it must be more interesting than a blank piece of parchment.

Carefully lifting up the inner lid of velvet Jac peered inside. Yes, it was definitely more interesting than the parchment. A small golden key, with a strange shaped end, lay nestled inside. He picked it up and just as his fingers were clear, the box snapped shut with a resounding bang. Jac frowned as he went to open the lid again but it would not open. He placed both the key and the parchment on the table and used both hands to try to pry it open but it remained firmly shut.

Well, he couldn't do anything. He certainly couldn't put them back if he couldn't open the box again so the custodian would have to look after them. He picked up the key and parchment again and steeled himself for the climb down. Usually if he had to go somewhere high he just told himself not to look down but that wouldn't work here as he had to look where he was going. It was a long slow climb and he could feel the sweat beading on his forehead by the time he reached the last few steps. His whole mind was focused on the next step ahead of him and he didn't even see the small group of people waiting at the bottom.

'Jac, can you fix this?' Dan shoved something soft at him but Jac was so shocked by hearing a voice unexpectedly that he took a step backwards and fell heavily on the steps.

Dan and Lotte leaned over his prone body, worried and anxious, their faces right up against his and Jac pushed them away. Then he saw Melanie was there too with a squirming Brad clutched firmly at her side. He sat up and then stood, wondering why she had followed him here. She had her hand covering Brad's mouth for which Jac was grateful as by the look in Brad's eyes he would have a lot to say on the subject of being carried around like he was.

'Jac, this is broken,' Dan held up the small bag that Jac had given him. 'Can you fix it?'

'In a minute, Dan. I need to find the custodian,' Jac said with a frown as he looked around for the little bald man. He could be anywhere in this huge room.

Before he even had a chance to decide how to find the custodian, Zora and Danel joined them.

'This lot might help,' Zora said absently as she held up a pile of tomes. 'What were you doing up there?'

'These were in a box up there,' Jac replied as he held out the two items for his mother to see.

'It's blank,' Zora commented with a look of slight surprise as she unfolded the parchment. 'What's the key for?'

'Beats me,' Jac replied. 'I thought I'd give it to the custodian to look after. I can't put them back in the box up there because it won't open again.'

'Maybe that means you should be the one to keep them?' Danel offered innocently and Jac frowned at him. He didn't want to keep hold of these things as he had enough mysteries to solve as it was.

'I could look after them for you if this wasn't broken,' Dan held up the bag again with a pitiful look of sadness in his eyes.

'Give it here,' Jac said with an exasperated sigh. The little puppet wasn't going to give up until he looked at it so he had better do it first. The bag was definitely not very well made as the cord that held it together was falling out. It would have to be re-threaded and Jac pulled on the cord to remove it so he could start it over and do it properly this time. Just as he flicked the cord free the material of the bag fell open to a single flat piece of hide and Jac stopped in mid motion. The inside of the bag was covered in lines and symbols. Jac stared at it as he dropped the cord.

'What's wrong?' Dan said almost jumping up and down, obviously worried that his bag had fallen apart.

'It's another map...' Jac said and Zora hurried over to look at it. 'Except this one looks different.'

'It's the real one!' Zora hissed in a whisper.

'It is?' Jac turned it upside down but it still looked wrong. 'How can you tell?'

'That square...' Zora leaned down and pointed to a small square at the bottom of the map. 'That's us. The star shape is the crystal. Watch the square.'

Jac stared at the map wondering what he was supposed to be looking at.

'Now move to your left,' Zora told him and he did, still watching the square. He had begun to think that this was silly, it was just a shape drawn on the hide, but then it moved. It was just a small movement but it was a movement.

'When the square and the star are on top of each other then we will find the Star Crystal,' Zora explained.

'So Ivan hasn't got the real one after all,' Danel said with a laugh. 'I'd like to have seen his face when he found out it was a fake.'

'First I have to fix that hole,' Jac said as he folded up the hide and shoved it into his pocket with a grim look on his face. He flicked a brief look in Melanie's direction. She was still standing perfectly still just beyond the others. 'Then we go and find the Star Crystal. As long as Gabbi doesn't find out we've got the map they won't try to take it from us.'

'My bag!' Dan cried softly as he watched his prized possession slip from sight. He bent down to pick up the discarded cord and held it possessively, glaring at them all, daring them to try and take it from him.

'I'll get you another bag,' Jac promised. 'This one's a bit too important for you to be carrying around.'

'What's going on here?' Trel asked as he and Gabbi arrived at the bottom of the stairs. Jac immediately slipped the key and parchment into his pocket with the map. For some reason he didn't want them to be seen.

'They've got a map!' Brad spat out as he fought his way free enough to talk. 'They kidnapped me you know. They can't keep me forever!'

Melanie muffled him again, her hand showing signs of dents from the little wooden teeth and Jac sighed. Why did that little troublemaker have to go and tell them?

'A map?' Gabbi asked, pushing her way through them all towards Jac. 'What map?'

'It's none of your business,' Danel said, stepping out to block her way.

Another voice solved the argument, at least for that moment, as it boomed across the Archives.

'The gifted one is down here. He must be taken before the council of elders.' It was the gatekeeper's voice and Jac looked sharply at Zora to see if he should be worried. The expression on her face was not what Jac had wanted to see.

'We've got to get out of here quickly,' she whispered and then pointed down the row of shelves. 'I know another way out.'

'They're over here!' Trel called out loudly as Jac, Danel, Zora and the two puppets hurried off through the Archives. Jac wanted to take Melanie too but Gabbi had moved in front of her.

'Why didn't Trel try to stop us with magic?' Jac asked as they followed Zora through many twists and turns. He was also worried about just leaving Melanie standing there with Brad.

'It's forbidden within the city,' Zora replied softly, turning again without hesitation. They arrived in an area that was very badly lit and the air smelled of dampness and rotting. Jac found himself thinking that tomes wouldn't last long in conditions like this and told himself that he had far more things to worry about than soggy tomes.

The façade of being a small building on the outside was so ridiculous that Jac laughed out loud and Zora shot him a warning look.

A soft click drew his attention to a dark recess and he realised with surprise that Zora had opened a door. Light flooded in and Jac shielded his eyes for a few seconds.

'Where does it bring us out?' Jac whispered as quietly as he could.

'In a back street near the edge of the city,' Zora replied softly. 'We won't be able to get back to the Flying Jug without being seen so we'll hide out in our old cottage.'

'Our old cottage?' Jac echoed under his breath. He had never even wondered where they had lived before joining the circus.

'Hopefully nobody will think to look there for a while at least,' Zora said with a hint of worry that made Jac nervous. He didn't want to think what the council of elders would do if they caught him.

Zora led them out into a deserted, narrow alleyway that ran between the back of two buildings. Nobody would guess that the plain green door led to the archives unless they knew about it. They wove their way through the streets, seeing only a couple of merchants, and finally reached a part of the town which looked to have been abandoned many years ago. Each cottage each had a small grassed yard in front of it but they were overgrown from years of neglect.

'Which one was it?' Danel asked as he hurried along, holding both puppets.

'That one,' Jac pointed to one that looked no different to the others but he knew it was the one.

'That's right,' Zora agreed, looking a little surprised. 'I didn't think you would remember it.'

They hurried long the badly cobbled street and through the garden. Zora pushed open a door and led them inside the cottage.

Jac followed, trying not to disturb the thick dust that covered everything. He had expected it to be empty but it was fully furnished, and even the kitchen table was set for a meal.

'We left in a hurry,' Zora said sadly. 'There wasn't time to take anything with us.'

Jac wandered around the room slowly and then stood looking out the dusty window as the others talked quietly behind him.

'Someone's coming,' Zora warned suddenly.

Jac moved back from the window and waited with the others at the far end of the room. He could hear a horse and wagon and they all waited for it to pass by but all of a sudden it stopped. A minute later a voice came from just outside the window.

'Jac?' A soft voice asked, and ended with a rise in pitch that turned it into a question.

Jac rushed over to the window and stared in wonder as he saw Melanie, standing outside, and his own wagon at the gate.

CHAPTER FIFTEEN
CHASING RAINBOWS

'Melanie?' Jac couldn't help staring and he opened the kitchen door and went outside. He didn't even checking to see if there was anyone else nearby. She looked at him with the still empty, staring gaze but deep inside he saw a stirring of life.

'Well, I never would have believed it,' Zora said as she too emerged from the cottage, followed by Danel and the puppets.

'Why does she look so familiar?' Jac asked.

'You played together when you were just a toddler.' Zora didn't quite meet his eyes and Jac turned back to Melanie.

'Is Tessa her mother?' Danel asked as he carried the two puppets towards the back of the wagon. They looked about to fall asleep and their eyes were barely open.

'No, I am.' Zora's face was expressionless as Jac turned to face her.

'You are?' Danel voiced the shock that Jac was feeling.

'I have a sister?' Jac stared at his mother and then at Melanie. He was trying to work out if she was older or younger when his mother finally replied.

'She's your twin. That's probably why you're both so drawn to each other.' Zora waited while Jac, and Danel, absorbed this new information before she continued. 'I had our cottage shielded so nobody could feel the magic from outside, but one afternoon Melanie wandered outside to play while I was asleep. It was purely bad luck that one of the council of elders came riding past while she played in the garden... If only I hadn't fallen asleep.'

Zora looked at Melanie with sad, sorrowful eyes. 'I knew then that it was going to be too hard to hide you in the city. I couldn't take Melanie as she would draw too much attention to us, so Tessa offered to take her in.'

Zora took Melanie's arm and led her after Danel. 'Put her on my bed in the wagon. She will be exhausted after the effort of coming here. It's not the same as it would be for you. Everything is ten times harder for her and just deciding to come to look for us should have been beyond her.'

'Brad isn't here,' Danel called from inside the wagon.

'I don't imagine there's much point in asking where he is,' Zora watched Melanie slowly climbing the steps of the wagon. 'We can't go back for him so he'll have to fend for himself for now.'

'Where to now?' Jac asked, knowing the answer as he climbed up to the driving seat. He would have liked to have looked around the cottage more, but he knew there wasn't time.

'We leave Mage City as quickly as possible,' Zora confirmed.

Within a few minutes they were free of the city buildings and heading out towards the wall. After a nervous half an hour Jac could see the walls up ahead in the distance but the people standing on them could be either the stone masons or guards, he couldn't tell from here.

'How close is the crystal?'

Jac pulled out the map, pushing the key and parchment back into his pocket, and looked at it. From what he had seen earlier it seemed a long way. Now, however, the map looked completely different. The Star Crystal symbol was almost right next to the square that Zora had said was them.

'I don't understand it,' Jac said as he showed the map to his mother. 'How can it move so quickly and what is moving it?'

'It's the nature of the spell that was set to keep it hidden from anyone except he who held the map,' Zora explained but her eyes lit up at how close it seemed. 'It moves every few hours. All we need now is to get out of the city walls,' Zora mused thoughtfully.

'How?' Jac stared up at the walls as they got closer, looking for any sign of the gatekeeper.

'It's not usually guarded on the way out,' Zora said. 'And hopefully they are still searching the city for us so they won't have thought to stop the drawbridge yet.

Jac sat silently as they rolled up slowly towards the walls. He realised that his mother was going slow on purpose, so as not to attract any attention, but it seemed to be taking forever. To his relief the drawbridge began to lower as soon as they were within a few wagon lengths of it and they drove out of Mage City totally unchallenged.

Zora flicked the reins and the horse trotted off, slowly picking up speed.

'Should I try to speed us up or am I still shielded?' Jac queried but Zora shook her head.

'No to both questions. You're not shielded but if you use your magic it will be easier for Trel to track you down and catch up to us, or Ivan as well.

Jac nodded, he had no desire for Ivan or Trel to catch up with them and they sat in silence as the wagon bounced steadily across the grassy plain, the swishing of the grass against the wagon almost lulling Jac to sleep.

'There it is!'

Zora's shout brought him fully awake with a

jolt. He quickly scanned the surrounding countryside, looking for what his mother had seen.

'Where?' Jac asked, confused, he couldn't see anything but grass in every direction. There wasn't even a tree to break the monotony.

'Over there,' Zora pointed off to the left but all Jac could see was a rainbow.

'The rainbow?'

'Does it look like rain to you?' Zora asked as she urged the horse to go faster.

Jac looked at the sky and realised that although there were a few clouds in the sky it wasn't raining.

'The crystal reflects the light from the sun and produces a rainbow. That's why it has to be moved every few hours or Ivan would have found it a long time ago.' Zora slapped he reins again but the horse was going as fast as it could.

'There!' Zora pointed to the rainbow and Jac could see that the grass was tinted with colours. The rainbow was directly ahead of them, so the Star Crystal must be there.

Jac looked at the map again and saw the symbols were on top of each other. They had found it. Jac shook his head in disbelief that they had found it so easily, it seemed too simple. As he looked at the map it changed. One second the symbols were joined and the next they were at opposite ends of the map. He looked up and saw the rainbow had gone.

No!' Zora cried as she relaxed her hold on the reins and let the horse run on, directly over where the crystal had been.

Jac stayed silent as the horse slowed down to a trot and then stopped altogether.

'Do we go after it?' Jac asked, not wanting to show her how far away it was now.

'No, we wait for it to come close again.' Zora jumped down and fetched a barrel of water that was strapped to the side of the wagon. She poured some into a large bowl and set it down for the horse. 'We'll head into Gullyville. I need some supplies.'

'Gullyville?' Danel had come from out the wagon to see what was going on. 'That's in the highlands.'

'So are we,' Zora replied. 'We have been since the mountain pass. The second pass was just a shortcut to get to the city.'

'So how come we've never seen the city before?' Jac asked, for they had travelled all over the highlands as far as he knew.

'You know that little stream we crossed up in the mountains?' Zora asked as she unhitched the horse and allowed it to wander free. 'As it comes down the mountain it gets bigger and down here it's known as the Wynderm. That's all that separates us from Gullyville.'

The Wynderm, that's all! Jac remembered sitting at the side of the great river when he was younger. Watching the swift current hurtling branches and leaves mercilessly downstream before the strong undercurrent sucked them out of sight forever.

He could see that Danel was thinking the same thing. How were they going to cross it? It was at least thirty feet wide and freezing cold, even in summer, and Jac had never heard of a bridge.

'Is there a bridge?' Jac asked as Zora squinted off into the distance. She was probably checking they weren't being followed. It was something that Jac hadn't even thought about and he knew he should have.

'There is if you know where to look.' Zora turned back, obviously satisfied that they were safe for now. 'We should make Gullyville by nightfall.'

They arrived at the Wynderm about halfway through the afternoon and both Jac and Danel looked suspiciously up and down the raging river. There was no bridge.

'We cross up here,' Zora said as she pulled the horse to a stop directly in front of the river where it tossed water high over a group of rough, jagged rocks.

'Here?' Jac and Danel spoke together. There

was no way the horse would go in there.

Zora ignored their protests and pulled a bright-blue sash from around her waist. She placed it over the horse's eyes and tied it firmly in place. She took hold of the horse's bridle and pulled it forward.

Slowly, reluctantly, the horse began moving forward. Jac watched as Zora's feet should have been plunging into the water yet they seemed to stop several inches above it. She wasn't walking on the water, she was walking above it. Jac looked closer, straining to see what she was standing on, and finally he saw a slight shimmer in the air. He worked his way out until he could see the edges of the invisible bridge but even though he could see it now he still didn't want to get down off the wagon. Just the thought of not being able to see what his feet were touching made him shiver.

Once they crossed to the other side his mother removed the binding from the horse's eyes and they continued their journey towards Gullyville. Jac checked the map every now and then but it didn't move much closer before they reached the elf town.

It was late afternoon when they rolled into town. It had started to rain an hour ago and they were all drenched. The streets were deserted as Zora drove the wagon up the main street and stopped outside the local tavern.

'Jac, take the others and get a room for the night. There's far too many of us to sleep in the wagon, besides it's too cold.' Zora picked up her large carpet-bag that she always kept under the seat and jumped down from the wagon. 'I've got some things to buy before the shopkeepers close up for the night.'

Jac didn't argue as she was right on all counts. There were too many of them and it was definitely cold. He shivered as he got down and went to open the back door of the wagon.

'What do you want?' A rough and unfriendly voice asked loudly.

A man stood outside the fancy double doors of the Inn. He was heavily built and from the looks of the scars on his face and arms he had been in more than a few fights in his life. He had his arms folded in front of him and he stood with a wide stance that suggested he was attempting to bar them entrance to the Inn.

'We need rooms for the night,' Jac said pleasantly. Antagonising this man was plainly not the way to go.

'The circus doesn't stay here.' Was the blunt reply as the man stared at Danel with undisguised dislike.

'We're not with the circus,' Danel corrected him but only earned a stare that would have made most people take three or four steps backwards. Here in the highlands things were turned around and the dwarves were disliked by the locals.

'We don't want your sort here. The circus is camped down by the town hall.' The man glared at them one more time and then went back inside the Inn, slamming the doors with a bang that almost splintered the wood.

'I guess we're not staying here tonight,' Jac said as he walked back to the driving seat. Danel joined him and they continued down the road, catching up with Zora as she was about to enter a shop.

'It seems the circus is in town too. We're going to have to stay down with them,' Jac told her when she raised an eyebrow in question.

She nodded briefly as they were all well used to the reaction of local folk. Everyone wanted to come and marvel at the circus but nobody wanted them actually in their homes or Inns.

The rain was still falling steadily and by the look of the heavy black clouds, which hung low in the sky, it would be raining for a long time yet.

They arrived at the field behind the town hall a few minutes later and the reception there was no better than it had been at the Inn. Several wagons had been parked a short distance apart and a large piece of canvas had been stretched between them, creating a small area where a fire struggled to stay alight. Most of the circus folk were sat huddled around the pathetic flames and none of them looked happy.

'I told you to keep away from the circus!' Mr Blyne literally jumped up from the campfire and strode out to challenge them.

'You can't stop us camping here,' Jac replied defensively. He was tired and cold and he wasn't in the mood to deal with the little dwarf.

'Just keep your distance,' the ringmaster ordered and shook his fist at Jac. 'If it weren't for you we'd still be in Sweetwater.'

Jac sighed as he flicked the reins and moved the wagon on without replying, he had no answer for that one. By the time he and Danel had parked the wagon a short distance away and set up the canvas lean-to on the side, Zora had returned with her purchases

'I don't think we'll have much luck getting a fire started,' Danel said as he piled wet wood into a circle of stones.

'There are some advantages to being an archmage,' Zora replied with a smile.

Suddenly the wood smoked and hissed, then burst into flames, instantly giving out a heat that could not have come from such wet wood. The ground dried out within a few minutes and Jac felt his toes tingle painfully as they warmed up.

'I'll get some soup on to cook,' Zora said as she

banged a few pots around and the smell of hot soup came far more quickly than it should. Jac wasn't going to question how as he was too hungry.

He went to the back of the wagon and found Melanie sitting calmly on the bed, wide-awake and looking far more alert than he had seen her so far. The puppets were playing happily on the floor, chasing a ball of wool like kittens.

'We're stopping here for the night,' Jac said as he held out his hand towards her and she stood up slowly. She did not reply but Jac had the feeling that she could understand him. Her eyes, while still distant, were not as empty, and he was sure he saw the hint of a smile touch her lips.

Dan and Lotte raced each other down the steps and Jac helped Melanie down and around to the fire. He briefly wondered where Brad was right now but he decided that the little puppet was probably just fine. He was probably tucked up in a nice dry corner of the archive.

'Did you see who was with the circus?' Zora asked as they ate. Everyone, except Melanie, paused in their eating. 'Princess Karlotte. It seems she did run away with the circus after all. Blyne seems to be having a hard time convincing her to go back home.'

Jac leaned out around the shelter of the canvas lean-to and squinted into the rain to see the circus' campfire. Sure enough the princess was sitting on a rock, looking miserable and wet with limp curls hanging about her face, while the ringmaster walked round and round her. From the way he was waving his arms he was obviously ranting on about why she should go home but the little princess didn't even look to be listening.

A chill ran down Jac's back again and this time he knew what it meant. He stood up and went out into the rain, staring out across the field and into the town. It was almost dusk but the darkness of Ivan's cape stood out clearly against the buildings. They stood and stared at each other for a full minute, rain pelting down unnoticed, then darkness fell and Ivan blended into the shadows.

'Come into the warmth,' Zora said as she pulled him back under the canvas.

'Ivan's here,' Jac told her.

'I know. I saw him in town. I don't think he knows we have the map yet, so he will probably leave us alone for now. He's just following to keep an eye on you,' Zora said in what was probably supposed to be a comforting tone but which made Jac shiver all over again.

They all fell asleep quickly that night, even the puppets who slept whenever they could, for as long as they could. Jac was finally having a dream that didn't involve crystals, maps or falling.

'The map!'

Jac sat bolt upright in bed, more angry at being snatched from a pleasant dream than anything else. Someone must just be having a nightmare for the map was still in his pocket. He put his hand in his pocket to reassure himself but he only felt the key and the parchment.

Zora lit a lamp and Jac saw Dan digging through his bedcovers.

'My bag!' Dan said as his search ended without success.

'What was it doing over there?' Jac asked the little puppet. 'It was in my pocket.'

'I just wanted to hold it for a while,' Dan answered in a small voice. 'And now it's gone.'

'Gone where?' Jac asked, exasperated and tired. All he wanted was a quiet night's sleep.

'Maybe it's on the floor?' Danel suggested as he rubbed his eyes sleepily.

Melanie was standing at the open door and she was pointing out it as she stared wordlessly at them all.

'I think she's trying to tell us something,' Zora said as she went over to the open door. 'There's someone running down the alley beside the town hall. I can only see a shadow but they're in a big hurry for this time of night.'

Without having to agree on what to do next they headed for the door and hurried across the wet field. Only Melanie and the puppets remained in the wagon.

Jac was the fastest, with Danel and Zora close behind him, as they raced through the dark alleyways and streets. Every few seconds they caught a glimpse of the thief's shadow and heard the odd clicking sound his shoes made as they closed in on him. Jac's first thought was that it was Ivan but they were keeping up with him too easily for it to be the archmage. All Ivan had to do was cast a spell and he would be miles away in a few seconds.

'This is a shortcut, Jac,' Danel called as he pulled Jac down a narrow alley. 'We'll cut him off at the end where it comes out by the river.'

Zora continued down the alleyway where the thief had gone and the two boys went to cut the thief off.

'Now all we have to do is wait here for whoever it is,' Jac said as they reached the end of the alley. Seconds later a small puppet appeared out of the depths of shadow in the alleyway.

'Brad!' Danel exclaimed.

Jac could see that the little puppet was carrying the map and he was hugging it closely.

'Give it back Brad,' Jac insisted but the puppet just sneered at him. 'What good is it to you?'

'It's no use to him,' a voice drawled from behind him and Jac spun to see Gabbi and Trel standing behind him. 'But we want it.'

Jac was still taking in the situation when Brad ran between Danel's legs and straight up to Gabbi.

'Thanks Brad,' Gabbi said, taking the map from him. She scooped up the puppet and just as Zora arrived on the scene a blanket of smoke rose up around them all.

CHAPTER SIXTEEN
THE STAR CRYSTAL

'Where are they?' Danel asked as the smoke cleared, leaving the three of them standing looking at an empty space.

'Remember that travelling spell I told you about?' Jac replied and Danel nodded.

'Why don't you see if you can reach Kimi?' Zora suggested as she turned and indicated that they might as well return to the wagon.

'Good idea,' Jac concentrated his thoughts on Kimi and to his great relief she answered almost instantly.

Gabbi has the map. Kimi spoke clearly in his mind so they couldn't be too far away. *I did not know they were coming or I would have warned you.*

'Where are you?' Jac spoke out loud as well as in his head.

Not far, a couple of hours out of town, Kimi replied. *Towards the Wynderm.*

'Thanks Kimi. Let me know if they move.' Jac relaxed a little. 'They're out near the river.'

'If we leave before dawn they won't get too much of a head start on us,' Zora said as they reached the wagon. 'We might as well try to get some sleep.'

Sleep was easier to say than find for the rest of

the night and Jac tossed and turned until he finally got up and stopped trying. He was worried he would sleep so heavily that he wouldn't hear Kimi if she tried to call him. Letting them get ahead again could have far more serious effects this time.

They were up and away from the town just as the first rays of light crept into the sky and they caught sight of Kimi's cage as Gabbi was leading the horse across the river.

The crystal has moved. Kimi's voice came strongly and so suddenly that Jac jumped. *It is very near.*

'The crystal is nearby,' Jac related Kimi's news to the others. They were all squashed up on the front seat as nobody had wanted to ride in the back.

As if to confirm his words, Gabbi jumped back up to her wagon and they raced off across the grassed plain. Jac kept them in sight as his mother led their own horse across the river and then they were racing after them.

Jac figured they wouldn't bother with trying to lay a false trail. With the crystal moving so frequently they would probably only have time to reach it by a direct line of travel.

'You know where this is heading, don't you?' Danel commented as Jac took the reins to relieve his mother after the first hour.

'The City,' Jac said with a sigh. He hadn't wanted to go near that place in a hurry and he doubted they would get a very good reception from the gatekeeper or the council of elders.

'Hopefully we'll reach the crystal before then,' Danel offered optimistically but nobody encouraged him. Chances were slim since they were only an hour out of the city and there was still no sign of the rainbow.

'Look!' Danel pointed off to the side of them and Jac turned to see what it was. Had the crystal moved? A large black horse was keeping pace with them, far off to their left. Ivan. He wasn't trying to go past them, seeming content to keep up with them and watch from a distance. It reminded Jac of the large black birds that hovered for a dead animal, hopeful of an easy meal. Ivan was little different in Jac's mind.

They finally saw the rainbow with ten minutes to go to the drawbridge and Jac's heart sank a little. The multi-coloured rays were arching directly into the walled city. The poor horse was looking exhausted but Zora did not let up the pace. The drawbridge would be opened for Trel and they had to get through it at the same time or all would be lost.

Sure enough the drawbridge began to lower as Trel's wagon stopped just short of it. Even from this distance Jac could hear snatches of conversation blowing on the wind. They were arguing over what the hurry was and Trel was not in a good mood.

Trel and Gabbi were just about across the drawbridge when Jac knew he would have to try to hurry the horse up. If they kept to this pace they wouldn't make it.

'Hold on,' Jac told the others as he wished hard that they would make it across the drawbridge in time. But the horse didn't speed up; in fact as far as Jac could tell… nothing had happened.

Jac watched Kimi's cage rattle over the drawbridge and disappear inside. He expected the drawbridge to rise, but it didn't. He exchanged a quick look at Zora as he could hear the gatekeeper cursing loudly to someone else.

'I said raise the drawbridge!' He leaned back out of sight for a second and then stared out at the wagon hurtling towards the city. 'What do you mean it won't move?'

Jac almost smiled. It was not the way he thought his magic would help, but he wasn't about to argue, it had worked and that was all that mattered.

Zora drove over the drawbridge at a pace that only a fool would have tried to stop her. Up ahead Gabbi and Trel were racing along the road and they were kicking up more dust than the last time.

Jac hoped the drawbridge would rise once they were across to prevent Ivan from following them but he heard the hoof beats of the great horse clearly even over the noise of their own wagon. With a thundering of hooves Ivan came up alongside the wagon and sneered at Jac.

'I'll be waiting for you… with the Star Crystal.' He didn't wait for a reply and his horse galloped ahead of them and increased its pace seemingly without any effort.

The rainbow was still well ahead of them. Jac squinted into the sun and saw it was half way up the mountain in the centre of the buildings. It couldn't have been in a much worse place, Jac thought to himself, but at least it meant it was hard for the others to reach as well.

Zora was urging the horse to speed up and the courageous animal was doing its best. When they reached the cobbled streets there seemed to be nobody about and Zora didn't miss out on the advantage of a straight run through the city. Without taking her eyes off the arching beam of coloured light she drove quickly through the deserted streets. Obviously people had already had to make way for Gabbi and Trel and they still peered from their doorways to see if it was safe to venture out yet.

They reached the middle of the city in just a few minutes and the end of the rainbow came almost within reach. Zora pulled up on the reins and the horse shuddered to a halt, shaking from its torturous run. The roads had been going up hill for the last few minutes and now they had arrived at the mountain. Just a few buildings were perched on the sides of the steep slopes and the road wound around the base of the huge rock.

'It's around this way,' Jac cried as he stumbled over a pile of rocks that lay in a heap at the side of the cobbled road. As they came around the side of the mountain Jac stopped suddenly and looked up in surprise. Half the mountain was gone. This must be where they were excavating stone for the walls. A tall slice of the mountain had been left standing on its own, well out from the rest of the broken and damaged mountainside. Several dozen sculptors were perched all over the rock, and even though it wasn't finished Jac could tell what it was destined to be.

It was a statue of a wizard, dressed in flowing robes, a staff in his right hand and a large broad-brimmed hat hanging low over his face. A long beard was swept over his shoulder by an invisible wind and his face was upturned to the sky. His left hand was stretched out before him, also raised to the sky, as if reaching out to catch something; and that was where the crystal rested.

It was at least several hundred feet straight up and Jac began to feel dizzy just looking up there.

Gabbi had wasted no time for she had already begun to climb the statue. Ivan was also climbing up, on the opposite side to Gabbi, and Jac rushed over beginning to look for footholds in the folds of the great cape.

The sculptors, seeing that their statue was being invaded, had slipped quickly down to the ground with an ease that made Jac jealous. He was almost up to the huge hand that held the staff and he doubled his efforts to come up level with Gabbi, receiving a glare as he matched her pace easily.

Jac realised there was a fourth person on the statue, Brad. By far the lightest of them, he was almost half way up the outstretched hand. There was little doubt that he would be the first to reach the crystal.

Jac, remember you can float. Kimi's voice was soft but insistent in his mind. He dared a glance down and saw that she was closed firmly in her cage. Gabbi was probably unsure where her loyalties lay these days and perhaps with good reason.

Jac hesitated for a second. Yes, he knew he could float, but floating a few feet above his bed was slightly different to being several hundred feet above a mass of broken rubble. He started climbing again but he realised that floating was his only chance of getting to it first. Taking a deep breath he concentrated on floating and was relieved when he started rising quickly up the statue. Ivan had also sped up and both he and the puppet were about to reach the outstretched hand.

Ivan, seeing his small opponent, reached out one hand and with a single sweep of his arm he knocked the puppet clear of the statue. The pause in Ivan's progress gave Jac just enough time to beat him to the crystal but the scream of the falling puppet was too much to ignore. Faced with an instant decision of whether to let the puppet fall and smash onto the stones below or not he realised he could not let it happen. Reaching out, he plucked Brad from the air but could not change his direction quick enough to reach the crystal as well.

Time seemed to stop for just an instant as Ivan grasped the palm-sized crystal and held it up triumphantly. Jac hovered in the air, forgetting for now that he was high above the ground, looking up to see what Ivan would do.

Far below them a crowd had gathered and they all gasped as Ivan, in his elation of having finally found the crystal, forgot where he was for an instant, and slipped. The crystal flew free from his grasp as he clung to the statue with both hands to steady himself. It arched out over the broken stones below. It was too far away for Jac to catch but, with a sudden push against Jac's chest, Brad leapt out towards the crystal. The little puppet grabbed hold of the crystal with both arms, spinning wildly as he was sent off balance, and then glared up at Jac.

'Well, catch me will you!' he called out almost hysterically.

Jac dove down at the puppet, not sure if he could get to him before they both struck the ground but Brad thumped heavily into his arms just a few feet from the ground and he pushed up into the air, only just missing the sharp rubble himself.

The gathered crowd stepped back several paces as Jac settled slowly to the ground. Zora and Danel rushed up to see if he was okay.

'I'm fine,' Jac assured them as he looked up to the top of the statue where Ivan had started to climb down with a look of pure hatred on his face. Gabbi didn't look very impressed either as she too came back down to the courtyard to join Trel.

'Halt! We cannot allow a gifted to wander free in the city!'

Everyone stopped and looked at the gatekeeper who was forcing his way through the crowds towards them. Behind him were seven smaller men, all old enough to have long white beards, and they also wore the same flowing white robes. Jac knew this must be the council of elders.

'Be careful Jac,' Zora placed herself beside her son and faced the men with him. 'Their magic combined might just be enough to overpower you.'

Jac put Brad down, still holding the crystal, and braced himself. He had no idea what to expect but he had survived this far and he wasn't going to back down now.

'He must be cleansed,' the gatekeeper announced loudly, seeming more confident with the council to back him. 'Who has the Star Crystal?'

Jac looked down at the little puppet. Would he hand it over?

'It belongs to me!' Trel came striding over to retrieve it from Brad.

'No! I must have it!' Ivan was only a step behind Trel and Brad looked nervously from one archmage to the other and then over at the council of elders.

Brad began to back away as the men came closer and just before the first one reached him he bent his little wooden knees and hefted the stone high into the air.

'Catch, Jac!' he called.

Jac reached out and caught the crystal with one hand, feeling a surge of power as his palm made contact with the star shaped gem.

'It's glowing,' Gabbi hissed at her grandfather as she grabbed hold of Trel's cloak.

Jac looked at his hand and saw that the crystal was glowing so brightly that the bones of his hand could be seen clearly through his skin.

The seven men of the council took action immediately. They formed a tight knot, raised their staffs together in the middle of the circle and the ground rocked with the clap of thunder that rose from them. They turned to point their staffs at Jac and a bolt of lightning shot directly at him. There was no time to think about moving out of the way and Jac's mouth fell open as he stared at the white-hot light that was speeding towards him.

He was thrown backwards by the force of the strike and he staggered three steps before he regained his balance. He stared down in wonder at his chest where the lightning had struck. Where was the hole, the burn, anything to show he had just been struck by lightning?

A fearful hiss of whispered horror rose up in the crowd who had crept back even further but remained watching. The council of elders were shocked and the colour drained from their faces. The crowd, seeing the confidence of their protectors had gone, began to panic.

'He'll kill us all!' a hysterical screech came from

the crowd, setting off a wave of panic that had people running in every direction, except towards Jac.

The council of elders had all dropped to their knees, heads bent low, and staffs thrown to the ground in surrender. Gabbi, Trel and Ivan had all backed away as well.

'Wait.' Another shout, louder than the rest of the babbling crowd, brought instant silence. Jac knew it was his mother without turning to see. 'What are you afraid of?'

'He is gifted.'

'The council could not strike him down.'

'He can kill us all!'

'Yes.' Zora held up a hand for silence. 'Yes, everything you say is true, but it doesn't mean he <u>will</u> harm you.'

An uncertain murmur swept the crowd.

'How do we know he won't?'

'Why should I?' Jac spoke out.

The crowd seemed to settle a little and the council of elders pulled themselves to their feet and retrieved their staffs, still looking nervous and worried.

'However.' Jac's voice brought instant silence. 'There is the matter of what you have done to all the gifted people in the past.'

Jac pointed to Melanie and then at another blank faced woman at the edge of the crowd who had not moved since the wagons had rushed along the streets.

'Jac,' Zora said softly as she shot him a warning glance.

'There are people trapped within those minds…' Jac stated firmly. 'They must be set free.'

The crowd shuffled uncertainly, ingrained mistrust and fear clear on their faces.

'We don't know how,' the smallest council elder stepped forward.

'I'll find a way,' Jac assured him.

'They must follow our rules… one rule for everyone.' Another elder spoke out.

'Of course,' Jac assured them.

'If you can find a way, you may free them.' The smallest elder stepped further forward and waved his staff to show his statement applied to all his fellow council members. The expression on his face clearly said that it was a decision made out of fear rather than understanding but for Jac it was enough for now. In time they would come to trust him.

'Thank you,' Jac said with a slight bow.

The council of elders melted back into the crowd who stared at Jac and the others for a few more minutes before going back to their business. Most gave him a wide berth though and soon the square was almost empty. Only two of the council elders remained, watching silently from as far away as possible.

'This isn't over yet,' Ivan, glowering with hatred, took a step towards Jac. He stared at the Star Crystal, reconsidered his position, spun on his heels and stormed off.

'Nothing good will come of this, Jac.' Gabbi was standing near her grandfather. 'It was all done for the best you know.'

Jac did not reply. He knew Gabbi would never change her mind so there was little point in trying to convince her. She walked back to her wagon and Jac realised there was something he could do to help someone else.

'Why do you keep Kimi locked up?' he called after her.

'So she doesn't fly off,' Gabbi replied hesitantly.

'But dragons are such good judges of character. Why should she fly away?' Jac asked.

'I...' Gabbi turned red and hurried off.

Jac sank down to relax against the statue. He balanced the Star Crystal in his palm, wondering what he should do with it. It seemed that it wouldn't disappear while he held it but would it relocate itself if he put it down?

Jac was more than a little surprised to see Brad still standing near the statue.

'Aren't you going with Gabbi?' Jac asked. 'Nobody is keeping you here and you seem more than capable of taking care of yourself.'

'I was hoping I could stay with you.' Brad's voice didn't have the aggressive edge to it any more.

'I guess there's always room for one more,' Jac said with a brief smile. Maybe there was hope for the little puppet after all.

'You took some of my tomes!'

An angry shout made Jac go instantly tense again and he looked up to see the custodian striding angrily towards Zora. Jac stood up and with his free hand he pulled the golden key out of his pocket.

'I meant to show this to you but we had to leave in a hurry,' Jac said as he intercepted the angry little man. He held out the key and the custodian stopped and stared in shock at it.

'Can I touch it?' he asked eagerly, his voice more like that of a small schoolchild than a grumpy old man and he seemed to have forgotten about his missing tomes.

'I don't see why not,' Jac replied. 'Do you know what it unlocks?'

'I certainly do.' The custodian picked up the key as if it was made of glass and then, hugging it to his chest, he turned and started to hurry off across the city.

CHAPTER SEVENTEEN
RAINING INK

They all followed the little old man across the square. Gabbi's wagon had driven off and Jac felt a stab of regret that he hadn't said goodbye to Kimi. He probably wouldn't see her again now.

'Hardly likely,' a voice above him said and he looked up to see Kimi hovering above him. 'Gabbi unlocked the cage.'

'Will you stay with her?' Jac asked as he hurried through the city streets, people parting before him and staring up at Kimi in fear.

'I haven't decided yet. Everything she did was because she believed in it.' Kimi flew up higher and disappeared over a roof but her voice added in his mind. *I'll think about it.*

They reached the Archives and the little man ran inside and over to the side wall. He stopped and waited for Jac and the others to catch up. His face was a picture of eagerness and delight.

The custodian was standing next to a large desk that looked to be built right out of the stone floor as no joins could be seen. The custodian moved around to the back of the desk and turned to face them. He held up the key and then pointed to the right hand corner of the stone desk. A small square of gleaming gold was inlaid on the stone and in the middle of that was a hole. Jac knew without checking that it was the exact same shape as the key for he had felt that shape so often in his pocket over the last day.

To Jac's surprise the custodian held out his hand and offered the key back to Jac.

'I think it's only fitting that you put the key in the lock,' he said.

Jac took the key wondering what it would do. His hand trembled slightly as he placed the key into the hole. With a final glance at everyone he turned it with one swift movement. He remained motionless for several seconds, listening for anything that might have happened. There were no great bangs or thuds, not even a click of the key in the lock.

Then he noticed that nobody was watching him any more. They had all turned to look at the wall next to the huge desk. Jac turned to join them and realised that part of the wall had gone, it hadn't opened or slid away into a recess somewhere, it had just gone. The huge arched opening led to a dark room and the musty smell of long trapped air was drifting out towards them.

'What's in there?' Danel asked. The most inquisitive of them all, he had already moved right next to it and was trying to peer into the room.

'I have no idea,' the custodian muttered, not

attempting to move any closer.

Danel had moved right into the middle of the arch and cautiously took the first step into the room. Nothing happened and he took another step, still nothing and he turned back to the others.

'It's too dark in here. We need candles.'

Comforted by the fact that Danel hadn't instantly turned to dust for entering the room; the custodian hurried over to a shelf and gathered a handful of candles. He handed them out and then lit them from another candle. Jac didn't take one as he still had the Star Crystal and its bright glow had settle down to a more gentle one.

Jac and Melanie entered together and suddenly the entire room lit up with the same lights as the main archive. They were just as dim as the ones outside the room but they seemed bright after the darkness.

'It seems to know when a gifted is in the room,' the custodian said in a hushed voice and looked all around the room as if he were being watched.

Jac had no idea what he expected to be in the room but he wasn't disappointed to see that it was full of more tomes on shelves. Not as many as the archive but still hundreds at least. Small stone tables, which seemed moulded from the floor, were dotted around the room and soft chairs were placed around them.

Jac switched the Star Crystal to his other hand. It wasn't heavy but it was annoying to have to carry it when he wanted to investigate the room. Here might lay the answers to all his questions.

'Jac,' Melanie spoke softly and Jac saw she had her hands outstretched and she was looking at the crystal. He didn't hesitate to hand it over. She wasn't going to run off with it and since she was gifted too it should not harm her.

What happened next was a complete surprise to Jac. As Melanie's hand touched the Star Crystal it glowed brighter again, making the lighting in the room seem as dim as the candles, and then slowly subsided back to a gentle glow.

'What happened?' Jac was ready to snatch back the crystal if it was harming Melanie but his mouth dropped open in surprise when he saw her grinning back at him.

'The crystal freed me.'

It was most he had heard her say and he simply smiled back at her, lost for words. Was that all he had to do to free the gifted?

'Zora.' He called over to his mother but she already had her head in a tome, seemingly unaware that anything else had happened.

'Jac, these explain all about your magic,' his mother held up a slim volume as she walked over towards them. Her eyes narrowed slightly as she took in the changed expression on Melanie's face, a look of pure relief washing over here face.

'I understood everything that was going on around me,' Melanie explained once they were all seated at one of the stone tables. 'It was just that it all seemed so far away. I couldn't seem to control my body properly. When you came,' she turned to face Jac with a smile, 'it was as if someone turned on a light at the end of a tunnel and I just kept running towards it.'

The rest of the day seemed to spin past so fast and Jac fell into bed at Tessa's with a huge sigh. Sleep came instantly and he awoke the next morning feeling refreshed and ready to take on the world if he had to. He found Melanie downstairs eating breakfast with a delighted Tessa fussing over her.

'Now don't over do things,' Tessa ordered as she filled Melanie's cup with more broth.

'I won't,' Melanie replied agreeably.

'Are you coming back to the reading room today?' Jac asked. They had agreed the room needed a name and it seemed an appropriate one.

'You couldn't keep me away,' she answered with a grin.

'There's still that hole to fix,' Zora commented as she joined them at the table. 'I imagine it's quite big by now.'

'Oh,' Jac had almost forgotten about it and he

blushed with embarrassment. 'I still don't know how.'

'Here,' Zora said as she handed him a thick volume, bound in black leather. 'I found it in the reading room just as we left last night.'

Jac took the tome and read the title on the cover.

'What to do when things go wrong... A beginner's guide!'

He grinned at his mother sheepishly for he had no doubt that this tome would come in very useful as he learned to use his magic. He flicked through the pages that were well dog-eared and worn. Obviously it had come in useful for a lot of people in the past as well.

*   *   *   *

A week later both he and Melanie stood in the middle of the reading room, concentrating on the latest spell they had mastered. It was an important one for without it Jac would have to travel all the way back to the lowlands to fix the hole.

'Good luck,' Zora called softly as a mist of smoke rose to engulf them.

The smoke cleared and Jac whistled softly to himself when he realised they were standing on a small hill overlooking Sweetwater.

'It worked!' Melanie seemed just as surprised. 'This is Sweetwater isn't it?'

Jac pointed down the hill to the huge black hole

that was by now ten times as big as when they left.

'I guess it is,' Melanie agreed. 'That's a good-sized hole. What were you trying to do?'

'Burn a bit of grass to frighten off some trolls,' Jac replied lamely. His attention was taken by a movement at the side of his vision. He turned to see what it was and realised it was the circus train coming down the mountain and they were heading for Sweetwater.

'I guess they convinced the princess to go back home,' Jac muttered. The last wagon caught his attention though and he stared at it for a full minute before he realised what he was looking at. 'Kimi?'

'Right here, Jac.' A voice came from directly above them.

Jac craned his neck up to look at the sky and saw his friend whirling and diving happily.

Gabbi agreed to go back to the circus. Kimi's voice was in his mind now as she soared almost out of sight. *I like the circus.*

Jac smiled up at his friend. She sounded happy and that was all that mattered. If Kimi was staying with Gabbi then she couldn't be as bad as she had seemed.

'Shouldn't you be fixing that?' Melanie brought his attention back to the hole.

Jac brought the tome out of his pocket and

flicked to the page he needed. He had been surprised to find a page that dealt with exactly what he needed and by the smudges and small tears on the edge of the page he wasn't the only one to have created a hole like this one.

Jac read from the tome, looking up every few words to see if it was doing anything. He breathed a sigh of relief as he finished the spell and the hole began to shrink. The river started to flow back down its regular path and Jac could almost hear the cheer from the dwarves as the hole disappeared completely.

'Goodbye Kimi,' Jac called up into the wind. 'Come visit sometime.'

Goodbye my friend.

Kimi's voice faded as the smoke came up to engulf them once more and when it cleared, the hillside showed only the dented blades of grass where they had been.

* * *

The view from the peak of Mt Vale was pretty in the last rays of the sunset. Jac thought it was the best place to come and think when life got hard. Freeing the gifted hadn't been as easy as it sounded for some had been lost for so long they were finding it hard to adjust to normal life again.

Both he and Melanie sat hugging their knees against the freezing cold wind that whipped their hair back and drove small drops of frozen rain at their faces. Perhaps the middle of winter wasn't the best time to be up on Mt Vale after all.

They both stood up, as they were up here for a reason, and the sooner they accomplished it the sooner they could go back to the nice warm fire of the reading room.

'Did you bring it?' Melanie asked as she arranged her golden robes about her.

'Of course I did,' Jac muttered. He fished into the hidden pocket of his blue robe and drew out the Star Crystal.

They held it between them and looked at each other to get the timing right. They would only get one chance to do this and they had to get it right.

'Three… two… one… NOW!' Jac called as they both heaved the Star Crystal up towards the sky.

They both began saying the spell that would break the crystal into thousands of pieces and cast it to the wandering winds.

At first, when all the gifted had been freed they had wanted to destroy it but they soon discovered that it could not be destroyed. So now they were making it into thousands of small crystals that would be of little use on their own. It was true that all of them would retain a small amount of magic but without all the other pieces they would never again be a threat to a gifted person or anyone else.

Jac let the last word of the spell ride the wind and they both looked up as the Star Crystal exploded into tiny pieces and then all the pieces vanished in a clap of thunder.

Jac drew out the other item that he had in his pocket. He had carried the blank parchment since he opened the box in the archives three winters ago.

Slowly, as if it were raining ink, the parchment became dotted with tiny marks and one small square.

'What should we do with the map?' Melanie asked as she looked at the newly formed map of the crystal fragments.

'I think I know,' Jac replied with a smile. He folded it in half and then held it up to show her. 'If I make holes down the sides it will make a nice bag and I know just the puppet who would want it.'

Circle of Dreams
Book 1: Runeweaver

All Zaine had to do was reach out a hand and he could take it. Sweat broke out on his forehead as he battled the desire to take the book. If he took it, his fate would be sealed.

He didn't want to be a runeweaver – but he did want to touch the book. He wanted it so badly that he found his hand stretching out to it even as his mind screamed not to…

The search is on for a new king or queen. The search is also on for runeweavers who can help contenders penetrate the Circle of Dreams and win the throne.

Zaine couldn't have chosen a more perilous time to discover his fate. For runeweavers must take centre stage in the battle for the new monarch.

He is destined to play a unique and dangerous role – to fulfil a prophecy that could spell great danger, and even death, for young Zaine.

Let the Contest begin!

Dragon Charmers
Book 1: Mountains of Fire

In a world where they can be sung into submission by dragon charmers – people have forgotten the true power of dragons...

Logan lives with Zared, an elderly, absent-minded wizard, in Shanoria – the Kingdom of the Dragons. His closest friend is Alyxa, a dragon charmer with the rare gift of soothing and commanding dragons.

But not all dragons are tame, and when feral Reds kidnap the crown prince, Logan and Alyxa are thrust into a fast-paced adventure and go in search of the heart of a dragon.

The Dragon's Apprentice

There's something odd about twelve year old Toby, and it's not just his purple eyes or his friendship with Klel, the dragon tied up in the castle courtyard.

He's been sacked from every job at the castle and being a page to the mysterious Prince Blaise is his last chance to avoid a cold winter in the poorhouse.

Then Toby learns a terrible secret that Blaise holds in a stone pendant and the prince's deadly plans for Klel. But Toby finds he has amazing skills that might just be able to help...

www.mcnabbnz.com

8198997R00123

Printed in Great Britain
by Amazon.co.uk, Ltd.,
Marston Gate.